I0587976

The Game and other stories

Joe Baldwin

For Christina

Copyright © 2021 Joe Baldwin

All rights reserved.

INFESTED

The blue lockers of Redhill High School were opened and slammed by the students in between the change of classes. The boisterous pre-teens conversed about different boys and girls of whom they found attractive, what they watched on TV last night, and what they were planning on doing after school when the weekend commenced.

She only girl who was not talking or even accessing her locker was Lindsay Graham. Lindsay carried all her schoolbooks inside her overstuffed bookbag, and the rest were stacked in her arms.

Lindsay walked through the sea of rich white kids, poverty stricken black kids, and the others. Lindsay was the rare poor white girl. Her family lived in the poverty neighborhood because her mother was a schoolteacher (at a different school, thankfully) and her father had been unemployed for years. And why the rich kids went to a public school instead of the nearby private school, which looked like Hogwarts and promised them a safe and great education, baffled her.

She left her Math class where Mrs. Simmons had given her a hard time for not participating during class.

"Just raise your hand; it's that simple, sweetheart. I know you know this. You've gotten an A on everything so far this year. But I will mark your final grade down for not participating," Mrs. Simmons said in a soft tone. The type of tone teachers used to show they were your friend. Or used words like "sweetheart," which Lindsay found to be cringeworthy.

But Lindsay only absentmindedly nodded her head. Her dark black hair was swinging in front of her face, covering her right eye. She shuffled out of the classroom so as not to be late for Mr. Barry's Science class.

When approaching the science room, she stopped. She wanted to turn around and sneak in through the opposite side of the hallway even if it made her late for class. But it didn't make a difference because the group of girls she was trying to maneuver around were in her class.

Rebecca, Morgan, and Emily were outside the science room, talking amongst themselves. Lindsay couldn't hear what they were saying, but they were laughing and tossing their blonde hair over their shoulders like they had told someone off.

Lindsay swallowed her fear and hoped they wouldn't bother her.

"Oh, hey, Linds," Rebecca said, chomping on a piece of gum.

Linds was a nickname her mother called her, and her mother was the only one allowed to call her that.

The three of them were equivalent to "the plastics" from the movie *Mean Girls*. Rebecca was the leader, and the other two followed her orders like soldiers. They wore essentially the same outfits. A tank top with a shimmery saying on them. A flowy skirt, which was way too short, and shoes with a high heel. They wore makeup mimicking real-life Barbie dolls. They never carried bookbags. They carried purses, but none of the teachers seemed to notice or care about any of that.

Every day, whether it was outside the classroom, in the hallways, or even outside her home, the evil trio made her life hell.

Lindsay ignored Rebecca's welcoming and continued into the classroom. Until she was pulled back out into the hall. Morgan had yanked the collar of her thin *Slipknot* tee shirt. She nearly lost her balance from her heavy bookbag, but the books she carried evened her out.

"I'm trying to be friendly with you here, Linds," Rebecca said.

The three girls joined hands, encircling her.

"Stop calling me that," she croaked in a small voice.

Rebecca rolled her eyes and said, "We were wondering what you were doing this weekend. What do you do in your free time, anyway?"

Lindsay jumped at the burr of the school bell, indicating the start of class. She tried to walk into the science room by breaking their Ring Around the Rosie, or in this case Lindsay. They bounced her frail body back into the middle of the cruel circle.

"She asked you a question," Morgan said.

If they were all redheads instead of dumb blondes, she would have thought they were attempting to steal her soul.

"Well, I guess I'm asking what you are doing tonight pacifically," Rebecca asked.

Lindsay so desperately wanted to correct her poor English but thought better of it.

"Studying," she said in a low voice.

"Great, so nothing important. We just wanted to—since you don't seem to get out much—invite you on a little adventure we're taking tonight."

"No," Lindsay said with a stern tone this time.

"But you didn't even hear what we are doing," Rebecca said.

"Ladies, class is starting now. Please come inside and don't make me ask twice. What are you girls doing, anyway?"

Lindsay experienced a wave of relief when she saw Mr. Barry poke his head out.

Rebecca turned to him and fluttered her fake eyelashes.

"Mr. Barry, we have created a love circle around Lindsay because we saw other kids being mean to her. We want her to know she is loved."

Mr. Barry released a long breath and said, "That's very nice, but class is starting now."

Fear struck Lindsay when Mr. Barry popped back inside to start class. He typically waited for all the students to enter before beginning. And not sitting at her desk on time gave her the worst anxiety.

"We're heading to Bronson's Peak for a little fun. You ever had vodka before?" Rebecca asked.

Lindsay wanted to crumble in front of them. She could hear Mr. Barry's deep voice starting his lesson on the periodic table, and she needed to be in class.

She slowly shook her head.

"Well, Emily's dad works at a liquor store and she got us some. So, if you want to be cool for at least one time in your life, join us tonight."

Lindsay had never wanted to be cool and still didn't. She only wanted to be the best student she could so she could make it to a good college in a couple of years. She already knew she wanted to do something associated with science because it was her best subject.

"Linds. We are waiting," Rebecca said in a sing-songy voice.

The books in Lindsay's hands were becoming unbearable to hold; she usually only carried them the few minutes between classes. And why hadn't Mr. Barry come back out here?

"No," Lindsay said and tried to run and duck under the arms of Emily and Morgan, only to trip and slide shoulder first into a locker. The four heavy textbooks sprawled out across the linoleum floor. Emily had stuck out her foot and tripped her.

Lindsay looked at all three girls smiling down on her.

"Then I guess you can watch where you're walking for the rest of the school year," Rebecca said.

"What is going on out here? Girls, get inside now." Mr. Barry peered at Lindsay on the floor. "Get off the ground and get inside, please."

The worst part was not over because for the entire class, she was forced to look at the back of Rebecca's big blonde oval head.

Lindsay didn't pay attention to the lesson. She was imagining an axe splitting Rebecca's head open, or a hand coming out of her balding spot like in *The Grudge*. She wished the worst upon her.

Luckily, Science was the last class of the day. When the final bell rang, she collected her belongings and ran out of the school the fastest she ever had. Rebecca and her posse stayed after to flirt with Mr. Barry so he wouldn't fail them for the year. But, after having Mr. Barry last year and this year, she knew he wouldn't fall for any of those tricks.

Lindsay did tell one lie to those girls, though. And it wasn't not wanting to hang with them. It was that she wasn't going home to study her Friday night away. Her plan was to do what she did every Friday night, enjoy a horror movie marathon. She began this tradition with herself three years ago and hadn't stopped since. She started with movies from the 1950s like *Creature from the Black Lagoon* and *Tarantula.* Currently she was on to more recent movies like *Get Out* and *Midsommar,* which she preferred.

As for tonight, she was planning a re-watch of the *Friday the 13th* franchise because, well, it was Friday, May 13th.

Lindsay lived only a few blocks from the school and walked home every day. She didn't mind except for the days the senior kids who had their licenses drove by her. There had been two instances of her walking along the side of the road and open bottles of soda being chucked at her head. One of the bottles exploded beside her, and she had to walk ten minutes in a sticky mess.

There were no such cruelties today as she entered her home in the same condition as when she left school. Her parents' place was a tad bigger than a studio apartment. Walking up the cracked cement front steps and avoiding the rusted tetanus-inducing railing was the first obstacle. Luckily, the books she carried forced her to avoid it. Once inside, her mother was next.

"Hi, Lindsey, how was school today?" her mother asked, placing a half-gallon of milk in the fridge.

Lindsay didn't look or acknowledge her; instead, she walked through the kitchen and to the hallway. To the right was the living room where her unmotivated, unemployed father slept in his recliner. The sound of his snores and the blaring TV showing the events of World War II were unbearable.

She shut herself in her adjacent room and locked the door. This was where she felt safe. This was where she could finally be herself with no judgement from anyone.

Posters featuring Freddy, Jason, and Michael Myers hung on the yellow wall above her twin sized bed. Slasher movies had a special place in her heart. Her dresser was to the left with a Zenith ten-inch television atop, which had gone out of production twenty years ago. But there was a VHS player included, so it was perfect for her older films she inherited from her aunt. On her mother's salary, they could only afford food and necessities.

Lindsay opened the bottom dresser drawer, and neatly stacked inside were paper cases, which held the fragile VHS tapes. She removed the first Friday the 13th film and placed it in the machine, which played surprisingly well. She lay on her bed, reached underneath, and pulled out a large bag of popcorn. She was relaxed to be with some of her favorite characters and getting lost in their world.

As she was loading the third movie, the doorbell rang. Lindsay ignored it until her mother pounded on her bedroom door.

"What, Mother?" Lindsay said.

"You have some friends visiting you." Her mother sounded joyous, maybe the most she had ever been. Her mother was always trying to get her to make friends, but Lindsay was more comfortable as a loner. Also, what friends would be—

Lindsay then knew who was at her front door. Those bitches really showed at her house.

"They are not my friends, Mom. Tell them to leave."

"Lindsay Pamela Graham, you get out here right now and talk with these girls who came all this way to see you."

Lindsay knew her mother wouldn't let up, and those girls wouldn't go away until she told them to, face to face.

She exited her room, and as she turned right, she could see the three of them wearing the same outfits they wore at school earlier. If her mom saw her in that outfit, she would call her a "no good slut whore," but Mom seemed fine with friends dressing in that manner.

"What do you want?" Lindsay said.

"We were just picking you up for our adventure," Rebecca said.

"And if you'll remember, I chose to decline your request."

"And if *you'll* remember, I insisted on you having a good time on a Friday night. I'm sure your mom would agree."

That made her blood boil because she knew what was coming next from her mother.

"How sweet of you ladies to do that for my Linds," her mother said.

Rebecca, Morgan, and Emily smiled in unison as though they had rehearsed it—which they probably did.

14

"The answer is still no. I'm busy."

"Well, I'm making the answer yes. Go to your room and get dressed, young lady," her mother said.

This argument would only go back and forth all night and Lindsay didn't have the bandwidth for that.

She stomped to her room and threw on a different loose band tee shirt and baggy black jeans. Then she reluctantly exited her home with her mother saying on their way out, "You ladies have fun."

Then begrudgingly, she climbed into a car with Rebecca driving, who was only sixteen years old.

"Uh, I'm going to guess you don't have a driver's license," Lindsay said.

"Chill your tits, Linds, I drive my mom's car all the time. Plus, it's only a five-minute drive from here."

She was a surprisingly safe and efficient driver. Lindsay assumed the ride in the back seat with Morgan would be an awful experience, but everyone was quiet the entire way there. The way she liked it.

When she exited the car, she wasn't sure where she was. She had seen this area from the road many times but had never been inside.

The four girls stood next to the blue sedan in an abandoned parking lot. In front of them was a lake. But it was a lake that appeared not to have been used in many years. The hole where the water usually was now looked black and grimy and dipped down thirty feet. Next to the hole was a tall tower with rungs climbing to the top of a fifty-foot structure.

"What is that thing?" Lindsay asked, curious about where this was leading.

"It used to be a diving board. They did outdoor contests when this was actually filled with water. Now c'mon," Rebecca said.

Lindsay watched as Rebecca, Morgan, and Emily tugged their skirts off their hips and dropped them to a puddle of cloth at their feet. Lindsay turned her head away, not wanting to see them in their undergarments.

"C'mon, Lindsay. You gotta take your clothes off. It's all part of it," Emily said, crossing her arms and pulling her tank top over her head. The others mimicked her.

Lindsay stood there with her arms crossed at her nonexistent bosom, holding her elbows. She was embarrassed, and even in mid-May, it was freezing at night in upstate New York.

In their respective bra and panties, the three girls began to climb the rungs. Lindsay remained at the bottom alone. She recognized she was stuck there. She could walk home, but it was dark, and she preferred the car ride.

Lindsay started up the rungs but left her clothes on.

They mocked her the entire way up.

"C'mon, Linds."

"You can do it."

"Why are your clothes still on? We don't have ours on?"

She made it to the top, which was a platform of five feet by five feet. Not enough room for four teen girls. Metal barriers were at each side, but the front was open where the divers used to jump.

"Okay, so who is going first?" Rebecca asked.

The other three girls looked away pretending they hadn't heard the question.

"Okay, no volunteers. That means we do rock, paper, scissors to figure it out," Rebecca said.

Lindsay halfheartedly joined the other three hands and put out scissors for the first round. The other three put out rock, like it was planned. All three pounded Lindsay's scissors.

"No worries, Linds. We always do two out of three," Rebecca said.

Lindsay attempted to trick the girls by placing scissors again, but again they all put fists out.

"That's not fair. You knew what I was going to put out," Lindsay said. It came out in a more aggravated tone than she anticipated. "I'm leaving. And I will walk home. There's no way I'm jumping into that filth down there."

Lindsay placed a foot on the top rung and her foot slipped off. She would have surely fallen to her death or serious injury if Morgan hadn't caught her arm. Morgan pulled her to the platform and tugged at her thin tee. It tore to shreds as the other two joined in.

The joyous laughter ramped up as they tugged at the crotch button and zipper of her jeans. They got the zipper down, and the baggy jeans were easily removed.

The laughter ceased when they recognized how bone thin Lindsay truly was. Her ribs were easily identifiable, and the bones in her arms and legs were almost transparent through her pale skin.

The red-lipped grin returned to Rebecca's face. "It's your time to shine, Lindsay. It's really not that bad. We've all done this jump before. It's a soft landing."

Lindsay stood with her heels on the platform just above the ladder, which would have been the worse way to fall the fifty feet. Beneath where she was teetering was hard packed sand. But the alternative of black filth didn't seem viable either.

Rebecca approached her and placed a warm hand between her shoulder blades. She guided her to the other end of the platform. The way a friend would help you into an unwanted date with a boy.

Rebecca sighed and said, "Okay, if you don't want to, we're not going to force you."

Relief washed over Lindsay and she loosened up.

"Did I ever tell you how we all became good friends?" Rebecca asked Lindsay. Lindsay shook her head. "Our parents. They all knew each other. And they all said the same thing about us while growing up. Isn't that funny? They said we were the most dishonest, untrustworthy kids they ever met."

Rebecca gave a strong shove to Lindsay's back. Morgan and Emily, as if Rebecca's shove wasn't enough, joined, pushing each of her bony arms and sending her off the platform.

As Lindsay sailed down, she didn't feel anger or fear. She felt relief. Wind blew her dark hair from her face, and it felt like she was flying. She was flying away from all her problems.

That was until she smacked the mud-like substance. The initial *thwack* of her small body hitting the muck forced the breath from her lungs. Then as she regained her breathing, she started to sink deeper.

The thick watery liquid filled her nose and the back of her throat. She attempted to lift herself, but she was being dragged back down like being trapped in quicksand. She panicked and kicked her arms and legs as if she were in a deep ocean, drowning. As she kicked, she discovered by swimming through with her arms out in front like a freestyle stroke, she was able to move. She pressed her lips and eyes closed, but something had already entered her. She couldn't pinpoint what it was, but it entered through her pores and other orifices. It felt like something was squiggling through her bloodstream and spreading to each corner of her body.

She finally made it out of the substance but still needed to crawl out of the deep dirt hole.

When she made it to the top, the first thing she noticed was Rebecca and her mother's car were gone, along with her two followers.

You made decisions in your life, and some are for the better. But most, like this one, like this entire night, were not. Her clothes were presumably at the top of the platform, but she didn't have the strength to climb. She didn't have the strength for much. But she began her slow walk home.

When she made it to her house, her mother was nowhere to be found. She typically went out with her girlfriends on Friday nights. Her father was in his normal position, snoring away on his recliner with the TV blaring.

Lindsay threw herself immediately in the shower. She turned it on its coldest setting and sat underneath the pounding water with her knees under her chin. She sobbed and remained there for thirty minutes. She sobbed like she had been violated, and that was exactly how she felt.

***

Lindsay woke in a panic. She pulled the heavy comforter from her torso and legs and ran out of her bedroom door and across the hall into the bathroom. She cupped her hands around the porcelain bowl and heaved out an orange and red liquid. It splashed against the sides of the toilet bowl, causing a blood spatter type look.

She investigated the white bowl, noticing some hair-thin, dark circular objects floating atop the poop water. She couldn't identify what they were, and they were encased in a white foam coating. She also had no intention of touching the odd material either.

She flushed the contents and returned to her bedroom. She pulled the black comforter back over herself, but it didn't relieve the cold shivers, which were constantly moving through her body. She couldn't stop the convulsions even with the space heater on full blast.

She fell asleep again and woke hours later to the sound of clinking pots and pans and a shouting match. She got up from her bed and had to catch her balance from the dizziness she experienced. She stood at her dresser, which had a small round mirror atop it, leaning against the wall. What she saw in the reflection was not herself. She looked even skinnier than usual, and her skin was nearly albino looking. Under her eyes were blue half-moon markings, which resembled bruising.

She opened her bedroom door as the shouting between her mother and father ceased with a slamming of the front door. Her father walked past her, mumbling to himself, and only glanced at her for a second before continuing back to his recliner. She hadn't heard what they were arguing about, but when they did fight, it was usually about money.

She did hear keywords such as "job" and "lazyass," so she could only assume that was it.

She heard her father stop and walk back toward her. He studied her face.

"Are you okay, honey? You don't look good," he said.

"I don't feel too good," Lindsay said, and her voice was so hoarse she could barely hear herself.

"I'm taking you to the doctor right now. Let's go."

He was out the door before her and starting his pickup truck. Lindsay was soon out the door after shrugging a jacket over her hoodie. She hopped into the truck.

"It's sixty degrees today," her father said.

"I know, I-I-I'm freezing."

He pulled out of the driveway and began the drive. Lindsay watched the houses go by in a blur, and she must've fallen asleep because she blinked and they were in a corporate park where their personal doctor was.

"Don't you ne-e-e-eed an appointment?" Lindsay asked.

"I'll make sure he sees you."

They entered the brown brick building and took the elevator to the third floor. They entered a small waiting room, which had chairs as an outer border and two tables with magazines strewn on top. Straight ahead was a glass window, which separated the receptionists from the patients. A woman behind the glass was typing on the computer, paying no attention to them.

"Sign the paper on the clipboard and have a seat, please," the woman said, not looking up.

Her father didn't sign the paper but knocked on the plexiglass window instead. The woman turned, and her thick blue eyeshadow, globs of mascara in her eyelashes, and heavy concealer to poorly cover her fine lines and wrinkles made her look like she was headed to the circus after this job.

"Sir, please sign the paper on the clipboard and have a seat. The doctor will be with you as soon as possible," makeup face said in a tone that showed she was annoyed but needed her job.

"My daughter is very sick and needs treatment right away," her father said. Lindsay had taken a seat in one of the green seats with no cushion. There were two other patients waiting to be seen. One was an older gentleman who was sitting on the edge of his seat, as if ready to be on the move, steadying himself with his cane. The other waiting patient was a middle-aged woman whose face Lindsay couldn't see because she held a *Vanity Fair* magazine there.

"Sir, if your daughter is that sick, I would advise you to go to the Emergency Room," the receptionist said to her father.

"I'm not going to sit in an emergency room and wait for hours before she is seen by a doctor. And I only trust Doctor Stevens' opinion anyway."

"Doctor Stevens is not here. He does not work on Saturdays."

The vein in the top of her father's balding head looked like it was going to pop. "I don't care which doctor is back there, give me somebody with medical expertise to tell me what is wrong with my fucking daughter."

Just then the door to the left of her father flung open, and a man in a white coat stepped into the waiting room.

"What is going on out h—"

The doctor paused when he spotted Lindsay.

"Ma'am, please step back here," the doctor said.

Lindsay stood and teetered a bit as the dizziness returned. She recovered and followed her dad and the doctor. She entered a room and sat on the cold examining table with the thin paper covering.

"Now I don't normally go out of line, but you look quite pale and dangerously thin. I am apprehensive to say that, since you could very well look this way all the time," the doctor said.

"I—I have always been skinny and pale, but it has gotten worse since yesterday," Lindsay said.

"What happened yesterday?" the doctor asked.

Lindsay didn't want to reveal what happened since she didn't want to think about it. She also didn't want to rat out the three girls because that would only equal more pain for her.

"I went for a walk yesterday and found this place I had never been before. It was dark and I made a wrong step, tumbling into a hole. At the bottom of the hole was this muddy liquid. I don't really know, but ever since then I've felt weird and horrible."

The doctor pushed the dark hair from his eyes and appeared to be considering her story. Her father was pacing the small examining room and pulling on his graying beard. Lindsay knew it was a nervous tic he had.

"I wouldn't really know what your condition is without conducting a few tests. Can I do that?"

Lindsay nodded her head in agreement. The doctor took her temperature, her blood pressure, and reflective tests in her arms and legs.

"Are you experiencing any nausea or vomiting?"

Lindsay shook her head. She wasn't sure why she lied to the doctor, but she did.

"Okay, that is good. Your blood pressure is low, but not a cause for concern. All other tests looked good as well. I could take a UGI test, and we may be able figure out what's going on," the doctor said.

"A what? What does that do? We're not all doctors here, doc," her father cut in.

"Apologies, sir. An Upper Gastrointestinal Endoscopy. It is a small camera that enters the esophagus and into the stomach so I can possibly see what is causing the rapid weight loss and work out a solution."

"A camera down her throat? You've lost your mind, doc. We're outta here. C'mon, we'll come back when Doctor Stevens is here. He actually knows what he's doing," her father said, yanking her arm. But she didn't move from the table. She wanted to do the examination, but she didn't like seeing her dad upset, even though his recent moods had been angry and sleepy. Lindsay guessed the argument with her mother earlier was the cause for this outburst.

Lindsay looked at the doctor, who stood there with a stoic look. She tried to read his face. She tried to will him to force her father to stay and go through with the test, but she knew medical procedures couldn't be forced upon anyone. And she was too young to make the decision on her own. Lindsay jumped from the table and followed her father out of the room.

When they got home, she ran directly to her room and stayed in her bed until the next day. All day Sunday, other than eating a few snacks and using the bathroom, she was in her room. Her mother came back on Sunday, and her parents talked like adults. And based on the moaning through the thin walls, they made up. But neither of them checked on her. She still felt feverish, had cold chills, and thought she looked skinnier by the hour, but she didn't vomit.

On Monday morning, she wanted to skip school, not only because she felt sick but because she didn't want to face Rebecca, Morgan, and Emily. Her mother yelled for her to get out of bed and into her car as she did every morning. Her father must've told her mother about the doctor visit, but either way, she didn't mention it or the way she looked the whole drive to school.

The school day was as normal as any other day. Lindsay remained quiet in her first three class periods as she usually did. What started to change was during lunch period. Lindsay was ravenously hungry, and the cafeteria had cheeseburgers. She ate four cheeseburgers and two orders of curly fries. She even knocked back a 32-ounce bottle of soda.

When she finished, she looked up, and the three girls were marching toward her empty lunch table. She expected a barrage of insults for eating so much and not gaining any weight.

They were staring her down, and they had those evil grins on their faces. But once they came within a few feet of her, their demeanors changed. Their smiles faded, and they turned back around to their lunch table. It was strange for the bullies to change their minds about bullying. But with every approaching step of the girls, there was a rumbling in the pit of her stomach. She was still starved, but it was more of an itchy, fluttering sensation.

She ignored the feeling and left her lonely lunch table. She always left earlier than everyone else so she could be on time for Mrs. Simmons's Math class. Unfortunately, she was forced to walk by the girl's table on her way out.

The itchy sensation ramped up when she passed them, and the feeling proceeded to her chest and throat. It was like she was going to puke in front of everybody and experience a heart attack at the same time.

She ran to the nearby bathroom, closed the stall door behind her, and heaved. All that came out was a black hair-thin line, which she had seen the first time she vomited. It was four inches long and bent in half. As she studied the mystery item, the feeling slid back down to her chest, stomach, and then disappeared. She wasn't going to reach into a toilet bowl, so she ignored it and flushed it. She wanted to go back for more food, but the bell rang, indicating the next class started in five minutes.

Mrs. Simmons's class was uneventful, and she told Lindsay to participate more as she did every class.

Now Lindsay needed to attend her least favorite class, not because of the subject matter but because all three of the girls were in that class. The only class she shared with them.

When she rounded the hallway corner, they were outside the classroom in their circle, gossiping as they usually did, but once they saw her, they scurried inside. There was no free torturing today from them. Not even a word to her.

Did they feel bad for what they did? Did they think I was going to tattle on them?

She entered the classroom as the bell rang so she didn't need to endure them for longer than she had to. Lindsay unzipped her bookbag and removed her science textbook. She experienced the itchy rumble in her lower stomach again.

Mr. Barry began class by instructing the students to open their textbooks. The rumblings reached her chest now, and her heart began drumming. She wanted to ask to use the restroom, but Mr. Barry was strict about bathroom use, especially so early to the start of class.

It reached her throat as it did at the end of lunch, and she was waiting for her body to throw her lunch all over her desk. She let out one short dry heave, but it dissipated. Instead, the itchiness turned toward her right shoulder. Instinct took over, and she scratched at it above the cloth of her hoodie.

When she scratched, there was a lump, like a water balloon under her skin. She tried to ignore it until the balloon travelled to her frail forearm. It was about the size of a softball. When it reached her wrist, she raised her hand and her sleeve slipped up her arm, exposing the growth.

"Mr. Barry, may I please use the—"

She stopped when the balloon split open in the middle like an eyeball. The split was tearing her skin, and a black hair-thin stick popped out. She recognized it as what she was extracting in the bathroom. Then a head pushed through. It looked like those beetles who had pinchers in the front of their mouth, only this insect was triple in size. Six more thin legs followed behind the creature.

"Oh my god, that is disgusting," the girl next to her muttered.

Rebecca flipped her head around and yelped at the sight of the bug.

Mr. Barry walked next to her desk as blood began dripping down Lindsay's outstretched arm and splattered onto the desk. The beetle creature crawled down her arm and jumped as wings fluttered above its body.

It flew and landed on Rebecca's forehead, crawling down the bridge of her nose. Students rose from their desks and exited the classroom like it was on fire.

Mr. Barry tried to keep everyone calm. The bug now balanced on Rebecca's heavily mascaraed eyelashes. The insect opened its pinchers and clamped on her eyelid. Rebecca attempted to swat at it, but it was clamped on tight. Blood ran like a river down her cheek as the bug fastened again. Then it hopped onto her cheek. Rebecca opened her eye, and her tear ducts produced a red liquid. She tried another swat, but she kept missing. The bug crawled to the corner of her reddened eyeball and used its pinchers to open the corner eye duct, then wriggled its way inside of her head. Rebecca let out a scream the whole school must've heard.

Another scream from another student brought Lindsay back to her own arm. Another bug was breaking through her skin. Then another. And soon they were marching out like soldiers. Rebecca collapsed on the floor in a spasm. Her eyes rolled back, leaving only white scleras. Blood leaked from her ears, eyes, and soon after, her mouth.

Mr. Barry was on his knees, performing lifesaving protocols and shouting instructions at students. The other beetle creatures weaved through the remaining students in the classroom who were too stunned to leave.

One landed on the frightened face of Morgan, who attempted to juke away from the bugs. But her attempts proved futile as they covered her face in a scuttering mask. They entered through her eye ducts, her ears, her mouth, and some skittered up into her skirt. It was all Lindsay had seen as Morgan ran out of the classroom and through the hall.

Other teachers entered the classroom, then quickly exited after seeing the blood and chaos. Lindsay lost track of the remaining beetle creatures but looked down at the exit point on her forearm. The wound closed and healed at a rapid speed. After the healing completed, she felt instantly better. The feverish feeling subsided, as did the shivers and hunger. She was her old self again.

Lindsay wandered into the hallway as though she were pulled there by some force. She turned left and away from the school's exit and the EMTs who were wheeling a gurney inside. She peered down at prone Morgan, who had not made it far from Mr. Barry's room.

Lindsay entered the girl's restroom at the end of the hallway to find Emily curled with her knees to her chin, her back against a stall door.

Lindsay knelt, and the blood was beginning its drip from Emily's eyes and ears as the beetles feasted on her insides. The bugs finished and strutted out of her nostrils and ear holes, fluttering their wings. The remaining beetles from the classroom joined. Twenty or so of them hovered in front of Lindsay's face. There was no fear as a few climbed on the bridge of her nose.

"Thank you," Lindsay whispered, and the swarm flew out of the restroom window.

She somehow knew they would return to their home in Bronson's Peak.

Lindsay exited the school and walked home with a big grin on her face.

BLACKOUT

Walter Stevenson sat beside his wife and daughter on the couch with a scalding mug of coffee in hand and the local news on TV. His typical nightly ritual. The recent happenings in the country—many of which had taken place in their own city—had been something he had wanted to keep his young daughter's eyes away from, but Sherrie believed it could be used as a learning tool.

When Walter was eight years old, the same as Shonda, he had been given "the talk." Not the birds and the bees, but the talk about being black in America and all that came with it. Walter had experienced much of what "the talk" entailed but was nervous to open that world to his only child.

The low whir of the desk fan at their feet, the local Channel 12 news anchor, and the balding, large white man, also known as Mayor Higgins, were the only sounds during the half-hour program. Mayor Higgins spoke on the riots and looting in response to injustice, and he gave a short, politicized speech, which only further divided the racial tensions. Then he continued for the remaining fifteen minutes about the rampant global pandemic.

"Time for bed, Shonda," Walter said.

"But it's only eight o'clock," Shonda retaliated.

"You have school early tomorrow. Bed now," Sherrie said with authority.

Walter always treated Shonda as Daddy's little girl, but Sherrie was the law of the land. She laid down the rules, and what she said went.

Shonda rolled her eyes, which her mother didn't see or chose to ignore, and stomped off to her room.

A few hours later, as they cuddled up on the couch, the first of the many cries for help came. It had always been a routine sound for the Washington Carver housing complex. They had had three homicides in the first five months of this year in their complex alone. Upon moving in, they were shaken by the first few gunshots and screams, which made their blood run cold, but after the next two, they chose to turn a blind eye. Especially when the police had given up on each investigation after only a couple of weeks. If they weren't showing any effort, then why should they?

"How is she gonna learn any discipline if you baby everything she does?" Walter received lectures from Sherrie nearly every night. "I want her to grow up to be a strong independent black woman. Okay?" Sherrie stroked Walter's thick dark beard and kissed his bald head. "Now—" Before she could continue, another muffled scream came, and this one sounded like it came from the apartment below them.

"That sounded like Kara," Sherrie said.

They had many dinners with their downstairs neighbor Kara Williams. She was elderly and lived on her own, so they handled any tasks she needed completed. Sherrie lifted herself from their bed and approached the front apartment door with Walter in tow.

"Don't go out there."

"I'm just looking." Sherrie peeked out of the peep hole and saw what she was expecting, an empty hallway. Then she unlatched the dead bolt and the dangling chain.

"Where are you going?" Walter was whispering now but wasn't sure why.

"I told you, I'm just going to take a look." She slowly opened the door and peered through the crack as another scream bounced off the walls. Sherrie slammed the door shut and locked it.

"Okay, this is not normal. Something serious is happening," Walter said. His voice quickened.

Sherrie stood there, bobbing her head. He could tell her mind was a million miles away, and she hadn't heard what he said. She had done this in many of their conversations. Then she muttered, "We need to help Ms. Kara. Stay here." Another yell—it sounded like a man's voice this time.

"No, Sherrie, you are not leaving this apartment. There could be somebody on a killing rampage."

"She needs our help. Keep watch on Shonda." Sherrie unlocked the door again and walked into the hallway. Walter ran to the open door, following, but stopped. He couldn't leave Shonda here by herself, but Sherrie could get herself killed. This was a possible life altering decision, choosing between his wife and child.

He walked back into the apartment and slammed the door shut. He opened side table drawers, checked the kitchen area, and searched the counter tops before finding the keys in his bedroom. He passed Shonda's room and knew he should tell her he would return soon and to stay in her room, but he believed it would be better if she slept through the ordeal and never knew about it.

Walter exited the apartment, keying the dead bolt before heading for the stairs. He assumed it was a positive when he didn't hear any more screaming, until he heard a familiar one as he reached the bottom floor.

"Sherrie." He ran to where the shriek came from and the open door of Kara Williams's apartment. His heart had left his chest, and it was solely beating against his temples. He held his hand out to open the door when he noticed the door had been caved inward.

With help from the faint twilight through the windows and a side table lamp, he saw the red blood spatter against the walls and carpet. In the wing backed chair sat a slumped body with a hardback novel on the floor in front of it. The gray hair and wrinkled body made him come to the realization it was Kara Williams.

"She's dead, Walter."

He jumped and nearly swung his fist around and clocked his wife. But stopped himself in time.

"Oh, Sherrie." He embraced her head as she collapsed to the ground. "Who did this?" he asked as though it were a valid question she could answer.

"I don't know, but I don't think it was a person."

At this, Walter looked over at Kara. He immediately saw what she meant. A large chunk was missing from the right side of her neck. As though a rabid dog had gotten loose. Although, a rabid dog could not split a door in half.

In this instant, he thought of Shonda all alone, protected by the same wood door, and a churn in his stomach assured him he made a terrible mistake.

"Well, let's not wait around to figure it out," he said, pulling her by her arms so she could find her balance.

They turned to leave, but a dark silhouette stood in the doorway. It looked human, or at least it used to be. The thing's leg was pointing in a ninety-degree angle away from its body, which caused it to stand like a broken bipod. As it stepped forward, it dragged its leg behind. It was a miracle the thing was even walking. And when the thing stumbled into the minimal light of the apartment, the red stains and tattered clothing made it clear it wasn't there to assist them.

"Elp meh," the mangled thing muttered through cracked lips. Its face had red skin indents that resembled pepperoni.

They weren't in a helping mood; they were looking for an escape route. "Plez, I don't wan ta do dis." It was as if it had marbles in its mouth. The thing scuddled toward them, and it moved quicker than either of them had anticipated. It leapt at Walter with its open jaw hanging so low it appeared unhinged, and razor-sharp teeth were prominent. Walter jumped to the right, causing the thing to fall to the floor and slide into a glass cabinet.

"Come on, you freak," Walter belted. The thing was to its feet and was scurrying toward Walter before he could motion for Sherrie to run, but she had gotten the message. The silent communication between husband and wife.

Walter made a juke he had done so many times when he played running back on his high school football team many years ago. A step to the right and a cut back to the left caused the thing to fall again, and Walter was out the door.

Sherrie was already to the stairwell at the end of the hall when Walter exited the apartment. He followed her with only one thing on his mind: Shonda.

They got back to their residence, and they both audibly gasped when the door had been busted inward, as Ms. Kara's had been.

As they entered, their eyes were not adjusted to the darkness.

"Check her room and I'll make sure that thing doesn't come in," he said. Sherrie concurred and disappeared down the narrow hall.

He couldn't be sure if it was from the events he had only now experienced or guilt from leaving his eight-year-old daughter alone, but he was visibly shaking, and a single tear dropped from his eye. He watched the tear fall into the palm of his hand when Sherrie's yelp forced his head to snap up.

"She not here. My God, where is sh—" Sherrie's voice cut off and went silent.

Walter crept with slow steps to the darkened hallway.

"Sherrie?" he said. Then a man the size of a professional football player emerged and locked Walter's head in a stranglehold. It was a dark arm with a large bicep, which was cutting blood circulation from his neck to his head. He clawed at the arm, but as he was lifted from the ground, he recognized there wasn't much fighting he could do.

As his mind faded to dark and the world became a blurry mess, he saw Sherrie's motionless body lying in the carpeted hallway.

***

The couch Walter woke on was one he could never afford. The smooth leather cool on the nape of his neck. When he opened his eyes, the blur that had been the last of what he saw had returned.

When the blur cleared, he saw a high white popcorn ceiling. He remained in the supine position he assumed he was placed into. He wasn't tied down, and he had a knowing in his gut that if he attempted an escape, the man who choked him out would make no effort to stop him.

All at once a flood of memories washed over him, and remaining here on this couch would accomplish nothing. The memories of earlier today—if it still was today—and the creature thing, which had removed the lovely Ms. Kara's jugular, flooded back.

His daughter.

Had he dreamt all of that?

He didn't think so.

Walter swung himself to a sitting position, and a wave of dizziness overtook him, causing him to nearly smack his head on the arm of the couch. When he caught himself and his eyes and mind were in full focus, he saw something he could have never imagined. Across from him was an identical couch where Sherrie lay with a light knitted blanket draped over her. Walter watched as her chest moved up and down and was relieved to know she was still alive.

The room they were in must have been a study of some kind, which appeared to be attached to a massive home. A large television hung above a stone fireplace, both of which were unused. A glass door that led to a hallway sat ajar with one large man sitting cross-legged in a recliner to its side. His gaze beamed on Walter.

"Good evening, Mr. Stevenson," the man in a gray three-piece suit said.

How did he know his name?

He patted the rear pocket of his jeans and understood this man had his wallet. When he studied the man, his large arms nearly tearing the suit, he was brought back to being choked out in his own apartment, and it triggered something in Walter.

Walter stood, found his balance, and ran at the man who had wished him a good evening. He clasped his hands around the man's lapels and threw him to the floor. The suit man was larger in muscle mass than Walter, but he used his dad bod to force him out of his fancy chair and to the floor. Once there, Walter began choking him.

"Where is my daughter, you sick fuck? Where the fuck is she?" Walter's grip on the man's neck grew tighter with every word he spoke. Killing somebody was not on his to-do list today, but Shonda trumped all.

Suit man was attempting to speak, but Walter was in a trance, and he wasn't sure he would come out of it. He did when there was a warm hand on his shoulder. Sherrie had awakened and was standing over him, looking like a zombie. Walter released his grip on the man and stood.

"You have a daughter?" suit man asked, trying to recover his voice back to its monotone state. This man was dark skinned, but to Walter he sounded like every white person he had ever met.

"Stop playing games with me. You broke down the door of my home and took my daughter. She's only eight, you freak." Walter had reached a level of rage he had not previously encountered but was calmed by his wife's presence.

"Mr. Stevenson, I assure you, your door was like that before I arrived, and there were no occupants inside your residence."

"Bullshit."

"I am only doing this to help you, Mr. Steven—"

"If you call me that one more time, I'm gonna flip my shit."

"Walter, if you hear me out for a moment, rest assured, you will understand."

Walter considered this. What could he possibly say that would detour his way of thinking at a time when his daughter was all he cared about?

"I may know who took your daughter."

Walter stood gaped at the man.

"Okay, I'm listening," Walter said.

***

"I'm Roger, by the way."

"You knocked us unconscious, took us from our home, and are holding us in this house, wherever the fuck this is. The last thing I wanna know is your name," Walter said, taking a seat back on the leather couch with Sherrie beside him, who looked in need of a drum of caffeine.

"I am in no way holding you captive here, Walter. Like I said before, I am helping you."

Walter gave a half-smile as if to say, *yeah, it sure didn't seem that way*, but motioned for Roger to continue.

Roger nodded. "I work at a major law firm downtown; I'm sure you've heard of it. Hanson & May. So, I hear all the goings on around the city. I overheard one of my co-workers who spoke to a client about an odd occurrence in their low-income housing. A strange creature that had killed multiple people in the complex. Our firm always accepted clients for shootings and stabbings frequently, but never large chunks missing of a person's flesh."

Walter immediately thought of Ms. Kara.

"The first thing I did was search online for anything related to these reports, but nothing came up. Even when I searched for the exact housing complex."

"The media usually doesn't care about us," Walter said.

"Right. Long story short, the next day I went to that complex and asked around. It was as if it never happened. As if they were being forced to keep it quiet. Even our firm dropped the case. As I walked through the halls, there was caution tape on multiple doors, but other than that, nothing. And before you ask, yes, I tried to gain access to the rooms. They appeared bolted shut with plywood, which only grew my suspicion.

"So, the next day I searched for other low-income neighborhoods in the city and came up with far too many. I decided upon one, which was far from civilization, as the other one was.

"I decided Washington Carver fit the bill. Lo and behold, it had some action. And it was scary to watch.

"I was set up across the street in my car. After waiting for three hours with nothing happening, I saw a police cruiser pull to the curb, and I noticed he already had somebody—something—in the back seat. The officer got out and opened the back door. A man—if you could call him that—exited, and his leg was mangled, like it was twisted in the wrong direction. The man thing ran into the building and, well, you know what happened next."

Sherrie shifted in her seat and appeared to be regaining her faculties.

"But the strangest thing happened before I entered. Seconds later, not enough time for anybody to recognize what was happening and call 911, an ambulance pulled behind the cruiser, and I watched as they entered with a stretcher. That's when I went inside. I was able to sneak past the EMTs without them seeing me. I have concluded that they will be doing the same to another housing complex in a few hours."

Walter swung behind him, noticing it was full dark. "How long have we been knocked out?" Walter asked.

Roger looked down at his hands as though he were embarrassed.

"You didn't call anybody?" Sherrie chimed in. "I mean about what you saw."

"Who would I have contacted? The police had initiated the mess."

"I don't know. What about the State Police, the FBI, the CIA, the president? Anybody else," Walter said.

Walter grabbed Sherrie's hand and pulled her to the exit. "We are leaving. Thank you for your hospitality, but

Mama always said not to trust strangers. Let's go." They moved through the threshold when Roger spoke again.

"Okay, I lied to you."

Walter whipped his head back. "What do you mean by that?"

"It was all true. Except that I followed close behind the EMT and watched them enter and exit your apartment. The medic guy busted in your door, which was how I got in there. They wheeled your daughter right past me. She was strapped down, and they were injecting her with something."

Like the devil awakening in the body of Sherrie Stevenson, she released a growl and leapt on Roger, bringing him to the ground. She gave two hard slaps—one to his right cheek and one to his left, and she would have continued if Walter hadn't pulled her off.

Roger dusted himself off as Walter held Sherrie by her arms. "Wasn't expecting to be tackled by a couple today, but it was well deserved. Let me clarify, I did not know that she was your daughter at the time. But I may have a way of finding her."

Walter was drawn back to Ms. Kara and the condition she had been in. And the thing that had attempted an attack on Sherrie and him. It lined up with what this Roger guy was talking about, but he wasn't sure he bought the "police attacking low-income housing" conspiracy theory. But, if he were wrong and his daughter ended up gone forever when he had a chance to get her back, he would never be able to forgive himself, and Roger might be their only lead to her.

"Okay, what do we do now? How do I find my Shonda?"

***

"How long are we s'pos to wait here?" Sherrie said into her cell phone.

"Until something happens, ma'am," Roger said through the phone's speakers.

She pressed the mute button and said, "Why are we trusting this guy again?"

Living in the places he did growing up and being surrounded by people the same color as him, he had always trusted his brothers and sisters. Sherrie grew up in the same neighborhood, where they met, but she had a different view on the subject. "He's the only lead to Shonda we have," Walter said solemnly.

"I hope you're right about this. She could be anywhere right now," Sherrie said.

"Do this with me tonight and then we can begin our own search for her. Okay?"

Sherrie crossed her arms under her small bosom and slumped in the passenger seat.

Hours passed and few words were exchanged between them when a voice jolted Sherrie out of sleep and Walter out of a wakened stupor.

"Police cruiser pulled up outside." It was Roger. He had Walter and Sherrie at a separate housing complex to cover all bases. "This looks like a hit. Hurry now. We are putting the plan into action. I'll take him out, then you guys head inside," Roger continued.

Walter flung his driver's side seat into the upright position, pulled the transmission lever into drive, and squealed out of the parallel parking spot. He was the most focused he had ever been in his life. And to his right, Sherrie looked frightened. He had never seen her scared of anything in their ten-year marriage.

"I'm going to move in and when you see the—" Roger said, then the phone let out three beeps and went black. Walter hadn't been keeping an eye on his phone's battery.

"Shit."

They were still a couple minutes away and their only communication was through the phone. "What the hell do we do now?" Sherrie sounded panicked.

"We get there ASAP," Walter said, stepping on the gas pedal.

When they were within one block, Walter cut the headlights off and brought the car to a stop beside a building that looked like it housed people at one time. "Okay, you stay here, and I'll see if Roger needs help," Walter said.

"No. I'm going with you. If I have a chance to save my own daughter, I'm taking it. Even if it takes my own life." Before Walter could protest, she was out of the car, already crouched, sneaking alongside the dilapidated building.

Walter followed close behind as they arrived at the corner where the police car sat in front of the brown brick building. It seemed every minute or so a screech would come from an open window and go silent. It was more frequent than when it happened at their building. It could only mean the death count was much larger. Whatever it was that was performing these killings was growing stronger.

Sherrie started toward the police cruiser like she was on a mission. Walter yanked her from below the yellow light of the cracked streetlamp, almost exposing them to the officer leaning on his car and smoking. They squatted behind a small green shrub, which was their only barrier between them and the cop.

They spotted Roger creeping across the deserted road, using his fingertips and feet to scurry across the double yellow line and place his back on the police car opposite of Officer Smoke. Walter made eye contact with Roger, who nodded, acknowledging his presence.

Roger looked like Rambo in his red bandana tied around his forehead and a ratty wife beater exposing his large arms and shoulders. Roger—on his hands and knees now—crawled to the front of the car and tapped the hood.

"What the fuck?" the officer said, blowing a plume of white smoke. Roger scurried to the rear and was behind the patrolman within seconds. In a mirror image to last night, but from a safer perspective, Roger grabbed the cop around the neck, and within seconds he was unconscious.

Roger dragged him back across the street, and as he disappeared into the mouth of an alleyway, an ambulance pulled behind the police cruiser and an EMT exited.

"Hm," the EMT said, looking around, presumably for his police friend. He shrugged and removed the gurney from the rear of the ambulance and rolled it inside. The screams were not letting up. It seemed they were going for a full sweep. Somebody had to get in there and help. As Walter mustered up his courage and was ready to fulfill the plan, he heard his name whispered.

45

Walter and Sherrie ran over to Roger and the unconscious officer.

"Okay, at least we took out the one with the weapon. However, he will become conscious momentarily. I will remain with him and do some interrogating while you two attempt to stop the threat." Sherrie knelt and pulled the service revolver from the officer's belt.

"Let's go." Sherrie was across the street before Walter even figured out what was happening.

They entered the front door and into chaos. Every door through the first hallway was smashed inward, and inside each apartment were streaks of blood on the walls and puddles seeping in the carpets. The EMT who entered moments before them had disappeared, but they were more focused on halting the death count.

"We need to follow the screams," Sherrie said and nearly on cue, a shriek came from above them. There were elevators in the lobby, but the stairs were faster. At each landing they could see the destruction of what the thing was leaving behind.

They touched the top floor three flights up, and the unsettling but familiar sound filled their ears. It was the same garbling, gnawing noise that the monster thing had made in Ms. Kara's apartment.

They saw the creature exit an apartment doorway and move to the neighboring flat to continue the devastation. They watched as the thing reared its head back and the door exploded on the first skull smash. It was much smaller than the one they had dealt with but seemed more powerful. They had no leg break, but the thing's arm appeared bent opposite of its natural bending direction.

"C'mon," Sherrie said, slowing her footsteps as they approached the hoarse screams of an older lady. He knew this wasn't the same creature from last night, but it was possibly involved in his daughter's abduction and that was motivation enough. He ripped the gun from Sherrie's hand.

"I'll take care of this," he said and stepped inside the small apartment. The thing was hunched over the tenant who wouldn't need to worry about rent anymore.

He approached the small kitchen area with the gun raised. Sherrie crouched in the living area and shielded her eyes.

The thing never leapt for him or made any indication it knew he was behind it. Walter pulled the trigger, and the thing's head exploded like a pin through a water balloon, releasing all its contents and splattering onto the refrigerator. Walter pulled again and another bullet pierced the thing's lower back. In the low light it didn't look like blood spurting from the thing, but a green goo.

It wasn't moving or snacking anymore, but Walter was in a different world. He approached the thing and placed the barrel to its already oozing head. Then it was as if he had been lifted from his world of rage back to the real world.

"No, please, no," Walter said, taking quick steps backward, bumping into a recliner and collapsing to the ground with his hand over his squealing mouth.

"What?" Sherrie said from the other room. She uncovered her eyes and approached the kitchen. She came to an abrupt halt as she must've seen what he saw.

It was a silver bracelet dangling from the dainty wrist of the thing. Gleaming in the moonlight were the letters "SS." They would recognize it anywhere. They had gotten it for Shonda for Christmas last year. Sherrie sat next to him, and they held each other and wept, but they knew they couldn't for long.

***

As they reached the ground floor, they heard a squealing noise approaching the front exit. It was the EMT wheeling the gurney out with a man strapped with restraints. The EMT had a needle in the man's arm with the plunger nearly all the way in. A green liquid disappeared into the helpless man's bicep. Before the EMT could plead, he had a hole in his forehead courtesy of Walter. They unstrapped the man, unsure of the consequences. But the man thanked them and ran off.

"What happened in there? I heard gunfire." Roger sounded panicked when they reached him. But the look on their faces explained the situation to him without saying a word. "Sorry. I did get some information out of him, though," Roger said, pointing to the police officer who had bruising forming around both eyes.

"What?" Walter sounded defeated.

"Well, it turns out that this isn't something the police force and medics have set up. This is coming from a higher authority." Roger paused, then said, "Mayor Higgins."

Walter and Sherrie shared puzzled looks. "How can you be sure?" Sherrie asked, her cheeks stained with streaks of tears.

"With this." Roger pulled an iPhone from his pocket. "I had Officer Morse here unlock his phone, and I called the contact under "Boss." Higgins answered the phone. He seemed to be expecting a call because he asked if the job was done. I tried to interrogate him, but once he recognized it wasn't his cop friend, he hung up."

"So, what do we do now?" she asked. "Go after him?"

Roger looked at the bloodied, unconscious cop, then back at Walter and Sherrie. "I'm going to guarantee they will be coming to us." On cue, a fury of sirens blared and echoed from a few blocks away.

"But what were they doing? What is their end goal?" Walter asked.

"Targeting low-income housing and eliminating everyone inside. That sounds like common sense to me. C'mon, We should go."

They exited the alleyway when Walter stopped. "No."

"What do mean, no?" Roger asked.

"We can't let them get away with this."

"They have an entire police force with a multitude of weaponry, and we have a revolver with maybe two rounds. We lose that fight every time," Roger said.

"Then I go down defending my brothers and sisters."

"This is suicide, Walter. Please come with us. We will get them back for this. It's guaranteed, but right now we need to go," Sherrie said.

Walter extended his arms to the mouth of the alley with the gun barrel at the end. Walter's emotions were pushing him toward killing every cop he saw like he did the EMT. But Sherrie was correct. They needed more firepower and more people.

Walter stuffed the gun into his rear waistband, and they exited the alleyway.

We'll round up the neighborhoods in the surrounding areas who haven't been hit. And we'll hit back. They are winning the current battle, but with a bit of help from our allies, we will indeed win this war.

THE GAME

The Crockers rarely fought with one another. They only fought when they were in the house for long periods of time, which was often. It's not that they had a phobia of leaving their home, but it was that they often didn't *want* to. They retrieved groceries and had gone out to their respective workplaces before they recently retired. They were most comfortable on the couch, reading a mystery novel or viewing a Netflix show. But now was one of those times they had been inside for far too long.

"Can you please stop doing this?" Shelly screamed from the kitchen.

Greg rolled his eyes.

"What did I do now?" he said, slapping the hardback he was reading on his lap.

"Leaving your trash on the countertop. Three feet from the trash can, you know, where trash goes." She was standing in the entryway between the kitchen and living room, holding a crumpled piece of plastic wrap.

"Well, then it's not too far for you to throw it away. And it's even easier with your mouth shut about it," he said with a firmness to his words.

Shelly stormed back into the kitchen, and he could hear the slam of the cabinet where the trash can was kept.

Greg continued the novel he was powering through but couldn't concentrate on the story. He had many arguments with his wife, and they had gotten to this point many times. Their remedy was typically to ignore each other until they ordered a pizza and had dinner together, but his small remainder of testosterone might have caused a larger argument than usual this time around.

Marie, Greg's ex-wife, who died of a heart attack seven years prior, would handle those situations differently. She would sit next to him and they would talk it out together as a team. "Two people against the problem, not one against the other," she said often.

Shelly and Greg had only been together one and a half years and would be married one year in a few days. It was strange for Greg to marry someone at sixty-one, but from the moment he laid his eyes on her, he knew. Now, he was fantasizing about being a bachelor again, but that passed. At his age, he had to take what he could get. Alas, the tension in a small space didn't help anybody.

He rolled his eyes again and walked up behind her.

He slid his hands around her waist as she wiped the counter clean with a dish rag.

"I'm sorry," he whispered into her ear.

She continued scrubbing the granite, ignoring him.

"I think it's this house," he continued. "I think we need to get out of it. It's consuming us and it will eat us alive if we don't escape."

She stopped scrubbing and spun around to face him.

"And go where? Do what?" she asked, throwing the rag onto her shoulder.

"How about a vacation?" he said, smiling. The lines in Shelley's face grew more profound. Showing her true age. He knew she loved vacationing, especially somewhere warm, as she had mentioned many times. As long as she was happy, it would make his life easier. "Happy wife, happy life," as they said.

"And where will you be getting the money for this vacation?"

"From our pension. And I have been saving up a bit of extra cash."

"I'm not using my pension money for a vacation."

"C'mon, we can just take a short one. A couple days. It won't cost too much. It could be an anniversary gift to ourselves."

Greg shuffled to his twenty-year-old laptop in his house slippers and checkered flannel pants, which were frayed on the bottom from being dragged on the ground for too long.

He opened his laptop and did a Google search for vacations. He was greeted with options for heading to Hawaii, for which they would need to fly across the entirety of the United States and then some. He was more interested in an Eastern Caribbean vacation. So that was what he searched for.

The top option was a two-night vacation on a tropical island. Shelly appeared to change her opinion fast since she sat next to him and pointed out which vacation spot looked nice to her.

He clicked the link and a website loaded, showing a blue ocean, which bled into a blue and magenta sky as far as could be seen. The picture looked to be taken on a beach with pink sand.

"Let's do that one," she said.

The black lettering read: TROPICAL VACATION FOR TWO.

And underneath in smaller font it read: $200 for two nights.

And under that he clicked: BOOK NOW.

***

Neither of them had been on an airplane before, and they were shaking in the terminal with their suitcases between their legs. When they entered the plane, they were greeted by a stewardess and a gentleman who looked to be the pilot.

They must have looked nervous because the pilot said, "It's going to be a nice easy two-hour flight. Nothing to worry about." He said it as if it were a general introduction, but he was staring down the old couple.

And it was an easy two-hour flight. The stewardess was kind and checked in with them periodically, having to interrupt Shelly, who had headphones on, listening to forest noises to calm her anxiety. But she was happy to be interrupted for cookies and received a pair of wings from the captain upon deplaning. Greg was equally anxious, but two episodes of *Law and Order* later, they were ready for landing.

In the Miami airport, there was a man in a full suit, which featured a black jacket, a white shirt underneath, and a black bowtie. He held a sign that read: THE CROCKERS. It was included with the vacation purchase. The man, who looked to be one of the *men in black*, greeted them and rolled their suitcases to a black Crown Victoria. Their suitcases were placed in the trunk, and they were in the rear seats—off to their destination.

They were relaxed to be in a vehicle in which the wheels stayed on the ground.

That was until the driver turned in to the entrance of a helipad.

"We—we are going in that?" Greg asked, swallowing his fear halfway through.

"Yes, sir. That is the only way to get onto the island. Unless, of course, you are a great swimmer," the driver said with a chuckle.

During the twenty-minute helicopter ride, Shelly had about four panic attacks, and Greg, who was trying to calm her, made about ten references to how it was like *Jurassic Park*. And when the chopper hovered above the island, it was. The water was as blue as the photo online and the sky just as clear. Trees were packed in like sardines on the small area of land, disguising anything that may have been happening inside.

***

When they knew they would officially be on land for the next two days, they could finally feel fully relaxed. They looked at each other and cracked a smile. They were guided through a large opening as the helicopter pulled away, and Shelly needed to hold her straw hat to her head.

The large wood entrance door to their private island was surrounded by green shrubbery, and when the doors, which must've been ten feet high, were opened, the party had started.

Caribbean music jammed on speakers, which were set up on stands inside the entrance. There were men inside in colorful shirts doing a shimmy dance. Greg glanced over to see a man about eight feet tall. His stilt legs were dressed in swanky pants that flowed in the cool ocean breeze. Shelly was grabbed by one of the gentlemen into a dance, and she tried her best to keep up with a twostep that didn't match the provided music.

They continued their walk through the welcome wagon of island folk. Their shoes were filled with sand already, but Shelly had removed hers, and Greg followed suit, feeling the pink floury sand between his toes.

They approached a row of huts, which looked to be built from straw, but once inside one, they saw it was made of solid steel. It was a quaint little private hut. It had two twin sized beds, and a toilet/sink combination, which only provided a thin curtain for privacy.

Greg fell onto the bed when there was a knock at the heavy wood door. Shelly opened it, and a man stood there with a bright yellow flowered shirt that sported a red parrot and matching shorts.

"Hello, my name is Alexander and I oversee the island's activities. And I want to be the first to officially welcome you." He placed his arms outstretched, expecting an embrace, and Shelly didn't know he would hug her until he wrapped his arms around her torso and squeezed.

"Oh my, thank you. I'm Shelly and this is my husband Greg," she said, pointing behind her as Greg peeled himself from the bed. Greg got a hug from Alexander as well.

"Are you two young folks celebrating your honeymoon?" Alexander said with a hearty laugh.

Being an elderly couple, it was typically an opening for people to make those types of jokes, but it was a kind of honeymoon since they never had one.

"Actually, it kind of is. We have been married a year tomorrow," Shelly said, returning a laugh.

"My god, congratulations to you two on your anniversary."

"And I still love her," Greg said, kissing Shelly on the cheek. However, Greg wasn't sure it was completely true.

Alexander spun around in joyful circles.

"Wonderful. Just wonderful. Now I have some business to talk about."

Greg placed his arm around Shelly's waist and looked attentive.

Alexander held a clipboard and said, "According to my records, you two have already made the payment, which is wonderful. But I just need you to sign on the dotted line to confirm."

He handed Greg the clipboard with a pen tied to it by a string. Greg swiped with his quick signature and handed it back over.

"Wonderful. I will keep this, and you take that, and we are all set." He handed Greg a receipt, which he didn't bother to look at. "If you need anything, anything at all, you come visit me or my partners at the office up the walk between the palm trees. Just follow the signs. Also, there is a phone next to the bed. Just hit zero and one of my team members will come running."

Greg and Shelly thanked Alexander as he exited, and they latched the door. Greg threw the receipt onto the ground so he could kiss his wife. They bounced onto one of the small beds and had fun for the next hour.

***

Shelly got out of bed to pull the curtain back so she could relieve herself. On her way there, Greg heard a crinkling sound under her feet. It was the receipt Alexander had given them. Greg panicked for a moment since he had a flashback of tossing it on the floor.

"Just because we aren't home doesn't mean you can make a mess," she said, holding the paper out, her other hand on her hip.

"I—I was going to pick it up. I swear." He was jumbling his words.

Then a smile cracked on her face and Greg released a sigh of relief. He figured they were on the path of ignoring each other for the remainder of vacation.

"Let's see what kind of extra fees they added that will surely damage our bank account." She studied the paper and her brows creased.

"This can't be right," she said, eyes fixed on the document.

Greg got up from the bed naked and snatched the paper from her hand.

"What the—what is this?" he said after looking it over.

The top of the paper read: THE GAME

Underneath it read: COMPLETE THESE TASKS IN ORDER

Followed by three tasks to complete.

1. FIND THE KEY
2. FIND THE DOOR IT ACCESSES
3. WIN

"What key? This is bullshit. I'm calling Alexander right now."

Greg snatched the phone on the side table and pressed "0."

"Hello, front desk. How may we help you?" a voice said in a thick Caribbean accent.

It was Alexander.

"Alexander, I think there has been some kind of mistake," he said, his breathing growing heavier.

"Mistake? I'm sorry. We will do anything we can to remedy your unhappy situation."

"You gave us a sheet that I signed off on of what I assumed was the receipt, but it was in fact something different. Something called 'the game.'"

"Ah, yes. It's a fun little scavenger hunt we like our guests to participate in. We hope you will," Alexander said with an inflection of excitement.

"Okay, but I would still like my receipt," Greg said.

"Oh, of course, Mister Greg, I will send one of my associates to you straight away."

Greg's breathing leveled out, and his free hand unclenched the fist he was holding.

"Thank you. But I still have so many questions about this game thing," Greg said.

"Of course. And once my associate arrives at your door, he can relieve all your concerns. As I said, it is only a fun activity we play here."

"Okay, well, that makes sense."

"Wonderful. I will be talking to you soon then. Goodbye."

The phone clicked and Greg sat on the edge of the pushed together beds.

"Well, what did he say?" Shelly inquired.

***

After an hour of waiting, there was no knock at their hut door, and the day was drifting away from them. Greg was walking around holding his cell phone in the air to see if there was any service. There was none.

"Who do you need to contact anyway?" Shelly asked.

"My Facebook feed. That's who."

"We only have the rest of today and the day tomorrow before we go back home, and I don't want to sit around in here like we would do at home," Shelly said to Greg, who threw his phone on the bedside table.

"You're right, let's go enjoy the beautiful weather."

They changed into their swimming suits, Greg with pink and blue tropical trunks, and Shelly with a solid pink one-piece. They draped the provided gray beach towels over their shoulders and were sweating profusely after only two steps out of the hut and into the soft sand.

"Howdy there, neighbors," said a man walking alongside a woman, both wearing friendly smiles. The man was wearing a black cowboy hat with white shark teeth like a crown around the rim. He had no shirt, and his round drooping stomach hid the waistband of his swim trunks. The woman beside him was thin with tanned skin and dark hair, which fell to her voluptuous chest. She appeared to be about twenty years younger than the man in the cowboy hat.

Shelly and Greg waved back, noticing the couple was white. Greg wasn't expecting to see another American and assumed they had the small island to themselves.

"Where you folks from? I reckon not from here, are ya?" the cowboy hat man said, approaching Greg freely.

"We come from a small city called Baltimore in Maryland."

The man cackled and slapped Greg on his shoulder. "That's a riot, man. A real riot. June and I are from the Lone Star State. Dallas, Texas. I bet y'all couldn't tell. Yee haw!" The man gave Greg another shoulder slap, and Greg was beginning to get irritated but wanted to remain civil.

"I'm Greg, and this is my wife, Shelly."

"Well, rootin' to meet ya both. This here is my beautiful girlfriend June, like the month." He pointed to a woman who Greg was having a hard time peeling his eyes from.

"And I'm Rich. Well, Sheriff Rich to ya folks. I protect the fine people of Dallas county. No worries, though, I ain't got my weapon on me. That y'all can see," he said and winked. His stomach jived as he bellowed a laugh and spun around, showing he wasn't packing.

"Well, thank you for keeping those people safe. That must be a tough job," Shelly said in a soft tone.

"Thanks a million, ma'am. I do what I can," he said, removing his hat, exposing his shimmering bald head, and bowed to her. "Now what were you folks about to venture out on?" he asked, placing his hat back on his head.

"Actually, I've got a question," Greg said and pulled the Velcro flap up, reaching into his thigh pocket. He removed the paper he received from the island folk and showed Rich and June, asking if they had received the same thing.

Recognition was immediate in his face. "Yes, sir. The man runnin' the place said it was a fun thing they did here. Like the campsites back in Texas with the bingo and the kickball. Their version or somethin' like that. I don't believe it's mandatory. But it is a bit strange if I do say so myself."

"Yeah. Thanks, we thought so too," Greg said. Greg watched June nod in agreement, but looked down as though she wasn't permitted to participate in the conversation. The couples continued to stand there staring at each other for another few seconds.

"It was great talkin' with y'all, but June and me are gonna soak up the sun before it moves west," Rich said and walked off. Greg couldn't help but notice for the first time the bottom of June's bikini was a thong, and her swaying ass mesmerized him until Shelly cut in.

"Ya know if ya take a picture, ya can jerk to it later if it weren't for ya erectile dysfunction. Ya hear that all right?" she said, impersonating the cowboy and slapping him on the shoulder. Greg tried to keep a straight angry face, but his lips curled into a smile.

They wandered past the large wood doors through which they entered. Beyond them was an open beach area where the sun was beating down and the water was blue and clear. On the way to find a private spot, they saw June and Rich making out in the sand and getting a little too PG-13.

Rich looked up at Greg and winked at him before going in for more. Shelly chose not to look at them. They picked a spot out of sight of the lovers located at the far end of the beach. They couldn't go any farther or they would walk off the island into the water. If they turned right, they would enter the forest of palm trees.

Shelly entered the water, and when she looked down, she was shocked to be able to see her feet, as she told Greg.

She fell back, creating a floating bed. Shelly was an excellent swimmer, but she was way past her prime. Greg could also swim, but since he had a pacemaker put in, it ended physical activity for him.

It was four years ago. Greg was at home on his fifty-seventh birthday, doing as he always did, reading on the couch at his bachelor home after his first wife had passed.

He read *Lord of the Flies* at least twice a year because it transported him back to his childhood. He had a group of friends whom he had hung around with and would get into all types of trouble. But luckily, he didn't tick anyone off enough to drop a boulder on his head.

He was getting to the part where Piggy met his ultimate demise when he had trouble catching his breath. He loved that part, but it never made him react in that way. His heart was thudding in his chest like a jackhammer. He reached for the landline on the tableside and called 911.

When he arrived at the hospital, the doctor informed Greg he had atrial fibrillation, which made the electrical signals that trigger your heartbeat "out of whack," as the doctor put it. He informed Greg he could live with this condition or have a small surgery to put in a pacemaker. Greg didn't want the surgery, but the doctor convinced him it was remarkably simple, and he would be out of the hospital and back on his feet in twenty-four hours. The doctor was correct, and it had been ticking away since the surgery.

***

"That's weird, don't you think?" Greg heard a voice and was trying to come back to where he was. There was a floury substance in his hands, and he was squinting at the sun beginning to hide beneath the ocean. He sat up and grunted at his wife.

"Oh, sorry, dear. Didn't realize you fell asleep. I was just saying, other than that other couple, it's only us here. Don't you think that's weird?"

"I was wondering that too," Greg said, pulling himself forward to a seated position. "But it could be an exclusive type of situation where they only allow a certain number of people at once."

"Yeah, maybe. But they have like ten of those huts."

"I don't know what to tell you, darling."

"I was just thinking out loud, I suppose. Wanna head back? I hear they bring food to your hut three times a day. Dinner is probably there already."

"Yeah, I'm starved."

On the walk back, they didn't see the Texas lovebirds. They must've taken it back to their private bed. Which was good for all eyes, Greg thought. Public displays of affection should be held in a private setting. Especially when taking things a bit too far.

When they trudged through the sand to their living quarters, Shelly jiggled the door handle.

"Do you have the key?" she asked.

Greg instinctively checked his hip pockets, which didn't exist on his bathing suit. Then he dropped his hand to the thigh Velcro pocket where there was only a sandy paper explaining THE GAME.

"You know, I don't think we were ever given a key. I didn't even think to ask since the door was wide open when we got here. I could break down the door if you want," Greg said, forming a crack-lipped smile.

"No, let's go to the office and ask to get into our room," Shelly said, ignoring Greg's playfulness.

They walked back to where they originally entered and plowed straight ahead, following a wooden sign pounded into the sand, pointing them in the direction of THE MAIN OFFICE.

The path was surrounded by palm trees and sand. They walked for ten minutes before they finally saw a small building a few hundred feet in the distance.

The size of the office was a bit bigger than the hut they were staying in and looked to them like the office of an old run-down motel. Shelly opened the glass door, and jingling bells sounded, hanging from the metal bar used for exiting. Inside was a pale counter that ran along the right side until the wall where there was a tabletop connected for the workers to enter and exit.

Alexander came immediately out from the back to the sound of the jangling. "Mister Greg. Miss Shellbey. How can I be of assistance to you?"

"We are locked out of our hut and need a key. You never gave us one," Greg said with a sense of pride. It had been a while since he had taken charge of a situation.

"Ah, my mistake, Mister Greg. We will remedy the situation. But I do have one question for you if that is okay."

Greg and Shelly stood there, staring and waiting for him to continue without a prompt. Greg lightly nodded for him to go on.

"Have you looked over the instructions?" Alexander offered, placing his palms on the chipped countertop.

Greg and Shelly were in synch with their brows furrowed. "I'm not following—" Then Greg remembered the paper in his pocket.

"The game, of course," Alexander said.

"Wait, so you're telling me the key we need to find in the game is the key to our own living space." Greg said looking over The Game's instructions again.

"Yes, Mister Greg. We like to think of it as an adventure for our couples. Our lovely couple of Mister Rich and Miss June have already started. You don't want to fall behind now."

Greg was left speechless, then found his words. But the words he chose were not pleasant ones. "Listen, we want to lay down, eat some food, and relax. Because that is what you do on vacation. Now I know you have some kind of master key that opens all doors. Just open our door and I won't bother you for the rest of the time I'm here."

Alexander released a long bellowing laugh. "Oh, Mister Greg. The game started once you stepped foot on my island. But it is a beautiful night tonight—as it is every night—so you could sleep on the beach. That is romantic, is it not?"

"This is bullshit. W-w-w—" Greg's anger was building. "We don't even know where to start looking."

"Oh, but I can give you a hint." Alexander's smile did not waver.

"Okay, what is it?"

"The waves are close by, but not in the ocean. They are green except for the autumn. For when you say goodbye and here, we have one hundred five. Step outside and you will see the answer in front of your eyes."

"It's a tree," Shelly said nonchalantly.

Greg approached the counter that divided Alexander and himself. "Look, I apologize for raising my voice. Shelly and I don't get out if the house much and this vacation is the first time we can really relax. Now we would like to either gain access to our room or be taken back to the airport." Greg paused, then said, "Please."

Alexander showed his gleaming white teeth and whispered, "Mister Greg, you don't have a choice in the matter."

Greg's stomach dropped and his anger returned. "Let's go Shel."

Greg pushed the handle of the door, and the jingle bells smacked the glass door, making a sound which left Greg curious if it had cracked, but he didn't much care.

"What kind of place is this?" Greg asked as they trudged through the sand searching for either a way out or the mysterious key.

"I don't know, but they are getting a poor review from me once we get off this forsaken island. Its fine for a place to have games, but guests shouldn't be forced participants."

Greg nodded. "Since we 'have no choice', lets shake some trees and see if anything falls out."

***

It seemed to become dark much earlier than it did in Baltimore, even though they were in the same time zone. They had no watch or phones—both in their living hut, which had no signal anyhow—but they figured it had to be about seven thirty. Almost an hour after leaving Alexander.

"You know there was one thing in his little riddle that didn't make sense," Greg said.

"The whole thing was pointless and made no sense," Shelly rebutted.

"Yes, and he said in autumn they aren't green. But these are palm trees. They don't change color."

"He had it memorized, so I imagine he says it to everybody who comes here, who are more than likely all Americans. And Americans experience the changing of the leaves."

"Unless you're in Southern California or an awful Florida resident," Greg said, shaking his twentieth tree. "Are these even what palm trees feel like? In my whole life I had never felt one. They feel almost fake."

"They do, but, like you, I've rarely left Baltimore, so they could feel and taste like sweaty armpits and I would believe anybody who told me."

Greg started to get tired and was shuffling his untied white sneakers with no socks through the sand, kicking large amounts into Shelly's ankles. She didn't say anything because she was doing the same, but she had nobody in front of her to get sandy. It became so dark they were only using the minimal moonlight and trees as their guiding path.

"I am so tired of walking and shaking these damn trees," Greg said.

"The plus side is that you stopped making that Steve Miller Band joke. If you haven't noticed in our year and a half, I don't have peaches. I have limes. And that's being generous to myself."

"Well, I happen to love your limes. They are squeezable and—"

"Sh, sh, sh, sh," Shelly said in rapid fire succession, and even through the darkness, Greg could see the panic in her eyes.

"What?" Greg was whispering now and wasn't sure why.

Shelly held her pointer finger at the end of her outstretched arm for Greg to stop walking. Greg stood still and shrugged his shoulders at her.

"I heard somebody walking," Shelly mouthed to Greg. "In the trees."

"It could be the other couple or Alexand—" Greg stopped when he heard the shuffling noise too.

"Who's out there?" Greg shouted. Shelly smacked him on the shoulder the hardest she had ever hit him. She held the finger over her pursed lips, then grabbed his arm.

They followed the sound into the forest of palm trees until they saw the outline of somebody.

"Hello?" Greg said. Then a deafening pop made them both jump and drop to the floor. They saw a figure approaching them with a small silver handgun; it was Rich. He wasn't in his signature cowboy hat.

"Oh, geez, I'm sorry, folks."

"You shot at us and all you say is sorry? The fuck is wrong with you?" Greg spat.

"Look, something ain't right about this place. Y'all need to find a way out. Right now. Ya hear?"

When Greg gained his faculties, he noticed Rich's body shaking, and he looked unable to control it. For being a sheriff, he would need composure to do his job, but he wasn't showing he had any now.

"What is happening? What did you see?" Greg asked.

"Where is your girlfriend?" Shelly cut in.

Rich dropped his head almost in defeat. "After we spoke with ya folks, we went back to that room we was staying in, but we was locked out. We went to the office, and they said we gotta find the key to get in. Then we walked around here for hours. We somehow got separated, and now she's lost somewhere."

"But if you're looking for her, why did you shoot at us? We could have been her," Greg said.

"Well, when I was wanderin' around out here by my lonesome, I heard some noises and I followed them, and somebody snatched me from behind. Luckily, I always keep my firearm on me. Got a holster in my swim trunks you folks couldn't see before. I pistol-whipped him, but not sure if I hit him good. He had a large hunting knife. One of those ones you carve animals with, so I took off runnin'."

"Did you see who it was? Was it Alexander?" Shelly asked.

"It was definitely a black man, but couldn't see his face. He had some kind of white paint on."

"Okay, what do we do now?" Greg asked, and they both stared at Rich for instructions.

"Me? No, I ain't in charge here. I'm going to get off this island, that's what I'm doing. And I highly recommend you folks do the same."

He stormed off, leaving Greg and Shelly dumbfounded.

They continued their walk through the trees, contemplating their options. They discussed swimming away to the next plot of land, but they were far too elderly for such activities. And with Greg's heart condition, he would cease to exist before any other land was spotted. They couldn't call anybody since they didn't have phones or service. And they were beginning to recognize that all of this was on purpose.

From behind, they heard feet padding heavily through the sand. They turned to see a black man with white face paint. He was moving toward them at a high rate of speed.

"Run, Greg. Run," Shelly said.

Shelly tripped and fell through the thick sand. Greg attempted to lift her. Shelly got to her knees. The man was closing in.

"Head back to the hut and break down the door and try to call on the phone," Shelly said in a frantic voice.

"That's not going to work. I have been checking for service since we got here. Don't you understand? Nothing here is in our favor. This is the game. This is their game."

A shiny object was in the man's hand, and Greg recognized it as the knife Rich had explained he saw. Greg wasn't going to win a fight with this man.

But he had to try.

Shelly was back on her feet and had begun to run ahead of him, and Greg tried to keep up. They were almost to the open beach area when Greg tripped over something. It wasn't a tree or the sand or his own feet as he often did. It was something attached to the foot of the tree. He heard the distinct sound of plastic cracking. The sound when you accidently stepped on a child's toy.

He turned, sitting on his hind end, looking at a small black device lying among the sand. He reached for it, and when he picked it up, he was looking at a circular reflective piece of glass. Realizing it was a camera lens, he tossed it away.

Shelly returned to him and attempted to lift him from his armpits to get him to his feet, but the man with the knife had already gotten to them. He stood over them as Greg struggled to find his balance. The man removed a brown wood baseball bat from his bright red baggy pants.

That got the couple to their feet, and they ran off together hand in hand, but the man was too quick for them. He raised the bat over his head while running after them. It came down on Shelly's shoulder and she fell to the ground. Greg turned and threw a punch, which landed on the man's cheek. He looked at his knuckles to see white paint now missing on the face of the bat-and-knife-wielding lunatic.

The punch didn't seem to faze the man at all. His head didn't even jerk back as Greg pictured it would. He had never punched anyone before, but based on the action movies he watched, the man should have been on the ground.

Greg gasped and reached out to help his wife, but after locking eyes with the crazed man, he made the decision to run. He didn't want to leave Shelly, but he had no choice.

He made it out to the open area where they had come in. The large doors leading to the ocean were closed, but beside them was the open ocean, which looked black in the full dark.

He ran through the sand and dove into the water. He had not taken swimming lessons when he was a wee tike but did his fair share of swimming back then. He did know the freestyle stroke and began windmilling his arms and fluttering his legs.

He knew he wouldn't be able to get far because he was out of shape and had a mechanical device assisting his heart rhythm. He lived a long life full of enriching moments of elation and dooming moments of dread just as any other human had experienced. Floating in the open water knowing he was in deep trouble was the one of those moments of dread. One of those moments where you knew deep down inside that your life was coming to a close.

He must've been swimming for at least ten minutes when he couldn't go any farther. His breaths were not coming as easy, and he was beginning to get that bad feeling again that his heart was on its last few beats.

He was also not sure if he was going in the correct direction due to the pitch blackness around him. Only the light from the moon reflected off the water.

He stopped and luckily knew how to tread water. He treaded and listening for anything that could point him in the direction of land that wasn't the island filled with madmen.

All he heard was his treading arms slopping the water on the surface to keep him afloat.

As he kicked his legs, there was something floating beneath him he was able to tap with his toes. He was able to suppress the surprised yell after touching an unknown object. He didn't want to possibly give away his location.

He relaxed himself and stroked the item with his toes, attempting to identify it. It was hard and smooth with two oval holes.

He grasped the thing with his feet and brought it to his hands. This time he couldn't keep his scream contained. A scream which he had held in for sixty-two years. It was young and without hoarseness. That was when the man came out of the water and grabbed him from behind, choking him until he lost consciousness. The human skull he had found in the water fell from his hands and gently floated to the bottom of the ocean.

***

Greg woke to a burning sensation in his throat. Three…four guys appeared from behind a group of trees. They were standing in haphazard positions with no shirts and red baggy pants. They all had white paint on their black faces. The designs varied from dots and dashes to lines and ran from their foreheads to around the chin to their chests and midsections. The immobility of his arms and legs was the thing that made him most fearful.

His arms were stretched over his head, and his legs were tied tightly together by thick brown rope. As he looked to his left, he saw Shelly tied in the same way. Only her chin was on her chest. Seeing the rope crisscrossed across her body made him choke up a bit, but he held it together when he saw Alexander walk out from the row of palm trees and join the crew.

Behind Alexander was another man with a large camera on his right shoulder. The kind news crews used for "Breaking News" reports. Attached to the camera was a seven-inch-by-seven-inch screen facing outward. It showed what was being recorded. At that moment it showed a compilation of clips of Greg and Shelly arriving at the island, relaxing on the beach, and being chased through the mess of trees.

Greg's eye was trained on Alexander, who was standing ten feet away and to the right.

He began.

"Welcome. All of you. To *The Game*. It is a little TV show that we put on for the people of the internet that takes place right here on my island. Now you are all probably wondering how this works. Well, it's simple. We have been secretly recording you from the time you arrived and will continue until your departure.

"We currently have a bit over one million people tuning in to the live broadcast. A new record for us!"

Greg was beginning to identify the group of men as the people who had welcomed Shelly and him into the island.

He pinpointed one of them as the man who had danced with Shelly.

"Now, all four of your backstories will be given to our audience, and our audience will decide who will die first, then second, then third. You Americans like democracy, yes?"

Greg snapped his head to the right when he heard there were four people, and he saw two more trees, which were perfectly aligned. Rich and June were also tied in the same way. Their arms stretched over their heads.

Alexander approached Rich with the towing cameraman over his shoulder. "We do our research on each one of you. We look at medical records. Family history." Alexander was walking along his row of victims and stopped at Greg. "We want to see who has led their life with passion and heart." He poked Greg in the center of his chest. "And who hasn't." Alexander snapped his head behind him at the sound of Rich's laughter.

"Is something funny, Mister Rich?" Alexander asked.

"Not yet, but it will be soon. Ya see, I made a small phone call from a satellite phone when I was bein' hunted in the forest. I bring it with me everywhere, especially to places like this. Be prepared. I used to be a boy scout, ya see. And called some reinforcements. And when they arrive, you gonna be dead."

"That is impossible. My island does not allow for outside communication, and your rooms are thoroughly searched for any such things."

"So, you have never heard of a satellite phone. And I am a man who knows how to hide things. Ya hear me?"

Alexander seemed to not be bothered by this and said, "It appears Mister Rich has volunteered to go first. Which is wonderful because we have video footage to show for you." Alexander pointed at Rich. "Please begin that footage."

It was unclear who Alexander was talking to, but the screen on the front of the camera switched from Rich's smiling face to the streets of Washington, D.C. It showed a group of armed militia men marching with assault rifles in hand and bulletproof vests on their shoulders. A variety of them carried American flags, "don't tread on me" flags, and confederate flags. It appeared to be shots from different news stations. And Rich was near the front, marching up the steps of the United States Capitol building.

"What does this have to do with anything? I'm fighting for my—"

"Quiet, please, this is my favorite part," Alexander interrupted.

The video showed Rich at a podium with the Capitol building in the background and his compatriots surrounding him in support. "The democratic government has taken away our freedoms, and now they want to take away our guns. We are here today demanding our constitutional rights not be taken away from us," Rich said on the small screen before it went black and returned to current Rich's face.

"I don't see what that's got to do with anythin'," Rich said.

"Yes, of course. I know you Americans like to fight for what's yours. Even stolen land."

"How do I know you haven't stolen this land?" Rich retorted.

Alexander smiled and got within inches of Rich's face. And said, "I don't see what that's got to do with anything."

Alexander moved down the line to June. "I cannot spend all night on you, Mister Rich. We are losing time and money. Next. Miss June Hill. We don't have any footage, but we know all about her business. Isn't that right, Mister Rich?" He shot a glare at Rich.

June had her chin on her chest since the moment Greg saw her on the tree. Through the darkness, he couldn't tell if she was breathing. That was, until Alexander slapped her across her face and her head shot up. She let out a few high-pitched screams, which made Alexander take a few steps back.

Greg heard moaning from his left. Shelly was waking. She opened her eyes. They went big, and she, too, screamed. Greg could hear the intense fear in her voice. Greg smiled at her to let her know he was there for her.

"Miss June runs a prostitution ring that Mister Rich was supposed to shut down while on duty, but instead decided to take her in and shower her with gifts and vacations. What do you think your wife and son would have to say about that?

"I know I don't like people who do something as lazy as have sex for money. Not to mention, the immorality of the situation." Alexander finished and walked over to Greg, stared at him for a second, and continued to Shelly.

"Leave her alone," Greg shouted.

"Miss Shelly. You were the hardest to find information on. You grew up in a poor household and worked hard to get to where you are now. It is very admirable. But I know something your husband probably does not know.

"In our digging, our team did find a charge against somebody you are familiar with. James Fielding—that is your father, is it not?" Shelly remained stoic and unmoved. "Fifty years ago, your father was low on money and decided to rob a jewelry store. He also thought it was a great idea to use his young daughter for his own gain. He sent you inside the store as a distraction, but it did not work, and an altercation occurred. Your father shot the owner of the store and smashed the cases to make away with millions of dollars' worth of jewels, which you helped carry. And you both got away with it. I should also mention that the inheritance money off which you are still living is from dirty money; am I correct about that?" Greg wished he could wipe the tears running down her cheeks.

"That's a lie and you know it," Greg shouted. He wasn't sure if it was or not, but the look on Shelly's face, and the way she slumped as much as the rope would allow, made him believe it was true.

"Well, she is your wife, so I will allow her to tell you, but not right now, because we are down to our last victim: you, Mister Greg."

"You have nothing on me."

Alexander returned with an I'm-better-than-you smile. "That's what you think, is it? Well, that is where you are incorrect. You are correct in the fact that you have done nothing illegal as these other people have."

"What have I done that is illegal?" Rich cut in.

Alexander barely glanced at him. "However, as much as you claim to love your wife, I think it is very wrong how much you have lied to her."

Greg's face became the color of a redbrick building. Shelly looked confused.

"Ah, so she does not know. Excellent. Miss Shelly. How many times during your short relationship were you away from your home?" Shelly remained silent. "Your silence makes it sound like a lot of times. And are you aware what Mister Greg was taking part in during your absence?"

Shelly spoke with a hoarse voice. "No, I'm not aware."

"Would you like to tell her, Mister Greg, or shall I?" Greg kept his head straight ahead and remained silent. "Then I will answer for you. As I said, we go through all that happens, even internet activity, and Mister Greg has an account at an internet site where women remove their clothes for payment. And Mister Greg is very fond of Jessb00bz18. Even an intimate one on one session." A gasp from Shelly made Greg jump and caused the tight ropes to move a bit. Then her tears returned.

"Now that I have effectively ruined your lives in front of"—Alexander paused and looked at the small screen—"two million viewers! I cannot believe it." Alexander stood, facing the camera lens away from the four tied victims. "Okay, it is now time to make your voice heard. A voting prompt will appear on your screen for who you want to die first. Remember, three will die and one will be released. Vote now."

"That's bullshit." Rich again. "Ya won't release nobody. Because they will go to the police and send them to this island."

"Very observant of you, Mister Rich; however, I have several snipers, undercovers working for me in the USA. Even some who are in the police departments. And they will track whoever is released. And they will kill anybody who goes to the police. I have released a number of victims, and I have not heard a word from any of them."

Greg wasn't listening to them; he was only watching the small screen where a bar chart with each one of their faces appeared under each bar. The chart was moving like a wave. Greg moved from first to last to first as the votes were calculated. Then a snapping sound played. The votes were in, and Rich was the highest bar by a lot.

"Oh, oh, oh, Mister Rich, it looks like the people have spoken. No electoral college can save you. You are the first to die. Please bring out the weapon of choice for Rich." One of the men came from the woods holding a silver, shiny axe with a wooden handle. It looked like the ones the firefighters used to break down doors.

"Mister Rich, thank you for playing the game. The method of death has been chosen beforehand by our group for each of your individual personalities. And we decided Mister Rich has a poor mind and big mouth. So…" Alexander finished and lifted the axe with both arms. He swung it in a sideways motion, cutting Rich at the neck. It must've been a clean cut through his throat and spine because his head rolled off his shoulders and plopped onto the sand face up. Greg watched in horror and could have sworn he still heard Rich protesting and saw his mouth moving.

"Okay, one down, two to go," Alexander said with a face of red splatters, which now added to his white paint. Blood was still squirting in a pulsating fountain from where Rich's head used to be. June appeared just strong enough to lift her head to the right and cry out in a wheeze at her lover's head plopping to the ground. Shelly forced her head the opposite way of the onslaught. It appeared she didn't want to witness what may come to her soon.

Alexander turned back to face the camera and spoke into it, "Okay, the next vote will begin now. Miss June, Mister Greg, or Miss Shelly. Who will die next?"

As he talked to his audience, Greg watched the three of the other island guys cut the rope where Rich's dead body stayed, and it plopped to the ground. His arms were stuck in the overhead position he was tied in.

One of the men used some excess rope to tie cinder blocks to his ankles, and they collectively dragged him out of sight. Greg imagined the poor man being tossed into the ocean. His head remained staring at Greg with a snarling grin.

Greg turned his attention to the screen where the three bar chart levels stopped with June at the top, but Greg was directly under hers.

"Oh. An awfully close one this time, but unfortunately, Miss June, it has been determined you are next to go."

Greg watched her and she had no reaction. He wasn't sure if they slipped her a sedative, but she looked mentally gone. Drool was hanging on a string from her bottom lip, and her eyes looked to be rolling in the back of her head.

"For Miss June's death, we have decided her deeds as a sex worker must not go unpunished. Please bring out the weapon of choice."

A man appeared, holding a black square box with a red and black wire dangling. At the end of the wires were gold clamps. Attached to the box was a black wire connected to an unseen power source. Alexander approached June and pulled a knife from his red baggy pants. He pulled her bathing suit top in the middle where it was held together and cut it. The top hung there only held by the thick brown rope. Her nipples now poked out.

The man placed the box on the floor and attached the two clamps to her left and right nipples, respectively.

"Okay, flip the switch," Alexander said, and his partner did that. June convulsed and released a terrifying scream. Her skin began to tear apart like somebody was cutting her with a knife throughout the entirety of her body. Her skin was blackening as though someone had thrown her in an oven. When she finally went limp after what felt like several long minutes, Alexander gave his partner a nod and he cut the battery off. When Greg couldn't stand it any longer he looked to Shelly for comfort. He saw her eyes closed and dirt-stained tears streamed down her cheeks. It was down to the two of them now and Greg saw she wanted to continue her life.

Like clockwork, the three men returned from the water and cut down June so she could, Greg imagined, meet the same cinder block fate.

"How exciting! We are down to our last two. And they are married, how adorable. Let's remember," he said, facing the camera. "Miss Shelly was a child when she aided her father in a murder, but she was aware of the crimes she was committing. She could have told Mommy.

"And we have Mister Greg, who was dishonest with his wife about having camera to camera contact with another woman. The time has come. Vote now."

Greg didn't watch the screen for the first time. He watched his wife, and she looked at him. He mouthed, "I love you." He cried for the first time in a while. She turned away from him in shame.

"Ah, the results are in," they heard Alexander say. "Miss Shelly. It looks like our audience does not like accessory to murders. For your death, we have decided—"

"No, stop," Greg shouted.

"Mister Greg, there is nothing you can say that will stop this. And you get to return to your home safely and enjoy the remainder of your life."

"No, I want to sacrifice myself instead of my wife. Kill me. Save her."

"No. Greg," Shelly said, sounding as though her breath was taken from her.

"Hmm, let me converse with my team about this," Alexander said and walked out of earshot, huddling with the other men.

"Greg, please don't do this. I don't want you to die. Please, it's something I have feared every day since I met you. We are not young people anymore. We are probably both going to die soon enough. But I said to myself that I was older and would do anything to die before you did."

Greg only shook his head. "You have family left. I have nobody but you. If you're gone, I—I wouldn't be alive anyway because I would kill—"

"It has been decided. After conferring with my associates, we have decided to accept Mister Greg's offer."

"Nooooo," Shelly exploded.

Alexander ignored her cries. "For Mister Greg's death, we have decided to take away what you don't have. Well, I'm sure you have it, but it is black in color. I am talking about your heart, of course. Please bring out the weapon of choice. This one was tough to get here in time. This was not one we had lying around."

Two men struggled to push the object through the sand. It was a large flat silver metal plate, sitting on wheels. When they turned it around, Greg could see an on/off switch and a black cord snaking through the sand.

"I do not even know if this can be accomplished, but I am quite excited about trying. Let's not wait around any longer. Switch it on," Alexander said.

The guy standing at the side flipped the switch on. The device didn't make any noise other than a low chittering sound. Greg wasn't even sure what this device was until he heard a few chinking noises as a few of the evil guys' rings slipped their fingers and attached to the flat metal piece. When Shelly lost her wedding and engagement ring was when the crying started for Greg.

Greg watched his chest begin to rise, but nothing else. The ropes were holding him in place. He took one more look at Shelly, and he was disappointed to see her looking away. He was pulled back to the memory of the past year and a half and how it was the best he'd felt about himself since his wife passed. He knew he should have tried better to make her happy. All the ups and downs they got through together as one. He wished to see her face one last time before he left, but he was only looking at her gray shoulder-length hair.

Greg's chest was at the point where it couldn't move any further out when he heard Alexander's voice.

"Shut that off. Do you hear that?" Alexander asked his associate.

Greg heard what he was talking about. It was the familiar sound of spinning helicopter blades. Was it the one from when they came in? But Alexander wouldn't be worried about somebody he knew.

"Quickly, go check it out." Greg watched the short man run with sand puffing behind as he went. He returned as fast as he left.

"It is the police from Texas, boss," he said.

Once Greg heard that, a wave of relief washed over him. Greg could see the wind from the chopper blowing sand in a tornado motion.

"Quick, get into the office and hide in the back closet. Forget about these two," Alexander said. He and his men ran out of sight to hide from the incoming authorities.

"We are saved. Can you believe that?" Greg said to Shelly. But he noticed Shelly didn't look excited. She was still facing away from him. Maybe she was in shock or wanted to see the police for herself.

Beyond the arch of trees, a man appeared in full tactical gear and carried a rifle across his chest. Greg was shocked when he wasn't followed by a group of similarly dressed men and women. He imagined Dallas didn't have a small department. Then he noticed something more striking. What he wore had no patches or insignias. It was a plain black Kevlar vest and no other equipment.

"Are y'all all right?" the man asked them. Greg gave a reluctant nod. "Okay, ladies first." He yanked the Velcro open chest pocket and removed a switch blade. He sawed the ropes Shelly was tied in, and he caught her in his arms.

When she found her sea legs, she looked at Greg. Her face contorted in a grin, and he knew something wasn't right.

"Oh, Greg," Shelly said, shaking her head in disappointment. "You really thought I was going to spend the rest of my short remaining life with some sorry sack of shit like you? Get fucking real. This man right here." She thumbed to her right at the older man with a gray goatee. "We have been married for forty years and have been doing this scheme for that long. We are rich from this, but we can't stop. Sorry sacks like you log into their dark web and pay to watch people like you get shredded to pieces. Say hi. They're watching." Greg turned to the red splotches and Rich's head remaining on the floor. "Oh, Rich and June. They're right here." The persons whom Greg knew as the couple from Texas walked out of the tree line. Rich looked a bit different. He still appeared around the same age, but he had a full head of stark white hair. His clothing was still stained with the fake blood. He walked past Greg and reclaimed his former head.

June looked about the same, but the knockers were reduced to oranges, and she was peeling prosthetic skin from herself.

"Everybody here are actors, and they fooled the hell out of you," Shelly said.

"But—"

"But their backstories are remarkably believable. Yes, they are. 'Rich' puts on his prosthetics and travels the country to build his character. Don't worry, those guys in D.C were as fooled by him as you were."

"I tricked 'em all," the man formally known as Rich said in his phony southern accent, which Greg felt stupid for falling for.

"Our island folks bring it together when I bring somebody by. Don't worry, they all get a piece of the pie."

Greg wasn't listening anymore. His mind was triggered with memories of the year and a half they were together, and all the minor doubts he had made sense now. Her rush to get married. The times she travelled for "work" for periods of time. The times she would be on the phone for hours with her "friends." Her willingness to go on this vacation. It was all coming to together now.

"So, since we had a preview, and with your chest on the rise, we now know this will work. Let's give the people what they want," Shelly shouted to a roar of applause. The island folk even reappeared to watch the spectacle.

"Three, two, one." Shelly stood to the left of the device and flipped the on switch. Greg could watch his own chest begin to pull forward. He saw the face of his first wife. Her loving touch, her sweet kisses, her addicting personality. He was finally going to be with her again. And that was all right with him.

HOOKED

Billy Thomas leaped from his bed and ran downstairs to the smell and sound of crackling bacon on a skillet. It was Saturday, and it was Billy's favorite day. No school, no band practice—which he despised—and no responsibilities.

"Billy, honey, please don't run in the house," his mother said.

It was an old house. Built in 1898. When the Thomas family first moved there twenty years ago, Billy was still ten years out from being born, but when he was old enough to understand such things, he referred to the house as the haunted house. Shirley assured Billy that there were no ghosts in the house, but Billy was hoping there were.

Last year, on the night of Billy's ninth birthday, his mother and he ventured out on a haunted ghost tour in the surrounding cities. Billy was excited to learn how many ghost sightings were so close by. The story that made him most overjoyed was the sighting through the woods in his own back yard.

In the rear of the colonial were miles of woodland. "Cheese," Billy had called them when he was little. "Green cheese."

Now Billy's pronunciation had grown, and so had his fascination for the ghost stories. The story through the woods his mother said was "malarkey," but Billy believed it.

The legend went that two people were walking through the woods, a girl and guy, and they were kissing. Billy knew what the storyteller actually meant but didn't care too much for those specifics. The two heard some sticks cracking and leaves rustling around them. They stood and saw a creature lurking in the shadows of the night. He was a large, burly man who had a hook for a hand. They ran out of the woods. The girl made it out, but the boy was never seen again.

Billy had gotten shivers from that story when he heard it last year. And since then, he had wanted to go searching for The Hookman. But, since then, his mother wouldn't allow him to set foot inside the woods.

Billy continued his Saturday by chomping on scrambled eggs and bacon for breakfast. Then he played on his PlayStation his mother had gotten him earlier in the month. He tried to argue in the store for the *Resident Evil* game, but she said it looked too gory from the pictures on the back of the box. She settled on *Crash Bandicoot*, and Billy reluctantly agreed. So, he smashed boxes and collected fruits until lunchtime. After lunch, he watched Nickelodeon and fell asleep on the couch to *Hey Arnold*.

He woke to the doorbell ringing and his mother saying, "I got it."

It turned out to be his friend and neighbor, Derek.

"Can Billy come out and play?" Derek asked Shirley.

Billy rubbed his eyes and noticed it getting dark outside. He wasn't sure of the time, but he was sure his mother wouldn't let him outside this time of night. Even on a Saturday.

Shirley tapped her chin for a few seconds. "Okay, but only for an hour and stay in the back yard. I will flicker the back light when I want you to—"

But Billy wasn't listening after "Okay." He rushed outside, and they ran giggling into the back yard.

"Tag, you're it," Derek said, slapping Billy on his shoulder and running in circles.

Billy got close behind him, but he was not as fast as Derek.

"C'mon, Tubs McGee, you can move faster than that." Derek constantly poked fun at Billy's chubbiness, but Billy only took it as friendly jabs. It also gave Billy motivation. He moved his feet faster and came down on Derek's back with his palm.

"Gotcha," Billy said with his hands on his knees, attempting to heave in oxygen.

Derek immediately tagged back. "Shouldn't stop moving in this game."

Derek ran off again, but this time into the woods. Billy stopped on the edge of the forest.

"My mom doesn't allow me to go in there," Billy said.

"Aww, your mommy still tells you what to do. You wittle baby."

Billy knew Derek was only trying to get under his skin and he was doing a good job of it. Billy's fists clenched, and his face was getting warm.

"Why don't you call your daddy back? He should be back with those cigarettes by now; it's only been five years," Derek said in a mocking voice.

Billy took off into the woods. He wasn't planning on tagging Derek; he was planning on tackling him and punching him in his stupid face.

Billy was impressed with his footwork. He leaped over large tree roots and any branches that blocked the haphazard dirt pathway.

He was catching up to Derek and could hear his childish snickering between his breaths. Derek's unzipped hoodie was blowing back in the wind, and his white sneakers were blinding. It was nearing September, and it wasn't cold enough for winter clothes yet. Billy watched Derek spread his arms like wings, and his hoodie flew into the air. Billy avoided it and it fell to the ground in a cloth puddle.

Billy kept his chase on him until Derek tripped on one of those large tree roots while he was turned around mocking Billy. He flew forward several feet before landing on the hard ground in a pile of leaves. He let out an agonizing scream. A deep scream for a ten-year-old. Billy knelt and when Derek turned over, he could see through his torn tee shirt that his shoulder had popped out of its socket. Billy had seen this before when his father was stringing up Christmas lights on the house and fell off the ladder. Billy was only four years old, but he couldn't get the vision of the shoulder not looking right out of his head.

"I'll go get my mom. Stay here," Billy said.

"You're just gonna leave me here?"

"I'll be fast."

When Billy turned back toward his house, he saw how dark it had gotten and how far from his house they were. But he needed to get help for his friend.

Billy made a sprint to his home. He tried to mimic the run he had done when chasing Derek, but he couldn't. That was an angry run, and this was a scared run. As he ran, he saw a blip of somebody or something to his right, but he couldn't bother with someone who decided to take a walk. There was an emergency.

He wouldn't bother with that person unless they ended up right in front of him, which was exactly what happened. He bumped into a bouncy round stomach. He fell to the ground, but his shoulders remained intact. He peered at a burly man with a long gray beard, which fell to his chest. But Billy couldn't help but notice the silver round hook hanging out of the man's jacket sleeve.

Billy forced himself to blink over and over as if he would wake from a dream. The man stepped toward him, but Billy climbed to his feet and ran back to where Derek was surely still on the ground.

Billy found Derek still lying there, but he was never getting up again. He had a deep slice across his throat. Blood had soaked his gray tee shirt, leaving a dark stain. And through his shirt and torso was a large "X."

As Billy moved toward him, he was suddenly being lifted off the ground. He kicked his feet and attempted to hit whoever was carrying him. The man stabbed his hook hand through the hood of Billy's hoodie and carried him in that manner for what felt like miles. Billy couldn't shake himself free of the tight sweatshirt and gave up the struggle halfway there.

They came to a small shed inconspicuously in the middle of the trees. The large man opened the small door and ducked down to enter. He transferred Billy through the same hole in his hoodie on a hook located inside the small shed. Billy was hung there like the man was hanging up his coat after a long day at the office.

The man had not said a word the entire time either. Billy had tried asking questions like "who are you?" and "what are doing with me?" He even tried, "Are you The Hookman from the stories?"

Billy surveyed the small room. There was a toilet in the far corner covered in brown dirt, a stained mattress next to that, and a wooden worktable with some kind of clamp hanging on the edge of its wood top. The hoodie was choking him, and he had to pull it forward to relieve the pain and breathe.

"Don't move, or hit me, or try to run away. I will kill you," The Hookman finally said. He had a heavy baritone voice.

When he approached, Billy could see the dried blood on the hook, confirming what he already knew. He killed Derek.

"Why did you kill my friend?" Billy asked.

"Because he was not a good kid. He wasn't your friend."

The Hookman used his normal hand to lift Billy off the hook and lay him on the worktable. Billy turned his head to watch him search for something in a plastic bucket. While he did that, Billy searched around the room for anything that could help him defeat this man. It seemed the only tools were the ones he was currently shuffling through.

"Aha," he heard the deep-voiced man say. He held a large silver axe with a dark wooden handle. Billy hadn't cried—he wasn't much of a crier—or screamed yet, but there was a climbing emotion in his throat as the man approached.

He guided Billy's left arm with his hook and stretched it off the table.

"Hold it there and do not move or we will have to do it again," The Hookman said.

He raised the axe with his normal right hand and Billy had to eliminate every instinct to draw it back to his chest. The axe came down, and Billy squeezed his eyes shut. He didn't want to see what would happen, but he felt it. The axe had cut him where his elbow bent; he knew it. When he opened his eyes, he couldn't believe the remaining nub with blood squirting out.

"Get up. Hurry."

Billy sat up, and a wave a dizziness took over, but he found his balance. He hopped to the floor as the man spun the table clamp. He dropped the axe and grabbed Billy's bicep, shoving it between the clamps. He spun the handle in one fell swoop, and it locked his remaining arm into place. The sputtering blood came to nearly a halt. The pain had caught up to Billy, and he began to weep.

The Hookman used his normal hand to grasp his hook and yanked. Billy expected to see blood squirt from the man's nub as his did, but none came. Billy watched a spike at the bottom of the hook appear from the man's remaining arm.

"You asked me earlier what I was doing with you. Well, people have told tales of me for years. They say I kill for fun. They say I have no heart. They even say I'm a made-up story. As you can tell, I am quite real. I was a kid like you. I had few friends and family. My Pops left when I was about your age. I lived in the house you live in now."

Billy widened his eyes and let out a whining sigh.

"Yeah, I loved that house and everyone in it. I had my momma and my sis. I loved them more than anything. But one day, I got into an argument with my sister and ran into the woods crying. I ran into a man with a hook for a hand. He told me he was dying and had chosen me to take over. He chose me because he thought at twelve years old, I should've learned to be an adult by then. Not crying like a baby. It was harsh, but he was right. Then he brought me to this shack and chopped my arm off and stuck this hook to my arm." He held it up. "Ever since then, I learned how to get food on my own, live on my own, and survive. Something I think you can learn very quickly."

He pulled a seat over and held a small box. He opened the box and pulled out a needle and thread. He threaded the needle and sewed Billy's arm together so the bleeding would stop for good.

"So, I can't see my mom ever again?" Billy asked.

"You can't see anybody ever again. What would people say to a kid with a hook for a hand? You would be national news. If somebody sees you, you will be forced to…well, you know." He took the safe side of his hook and dragged it across his throat.

Billy began to snuffle and cry at the thought of never seeing his mother again.

"I know. It was hard for me at first, too. But the reality of it is that she will die sooner or later. And since you know where she lives, you will be able to protect her. I used to stand just inside the wooded area and watch your mother through the window, reading a book or even sleeping."

Billy wiped his tears and snot with his good hand and asked, "But why does there have to be a Hookman? Sorry if this offends you, but—"

He released a hearty laugh. "I have learned to let nothing bother me; it is better that way."

Billy nodded. "Why can't after you die, it just ends? Like no more Hookman."

He smiled. "You asked the same questions I did when I started. The reason the Hookman story is so widely known is because there is one in most cities in the United States. We protect people from violence, and we rid the bad in the world. If there wasn't us"—he pointed his hook at himself and Billy—"there would be more bad people in this world. The story you probably heard was the couple havin' intercourse in this very forest."

Billy nodded.

"Well, the real story was that man was in this forest to kill her. I came upon them when he began to choke her. I stuck my hook through his throat, and it came out of his spine. The girl probably saw me, but I wouldn't kill her anyhow. Because even if somebody sees ya, doesn't mean they figured you out. It revamps the old wives' tale."

"So, why are you done, are you—are you dying?" Billy asked.

"Yup, I can't see no doctor, but imagine I got some intestinal thing goin' on." He lifted his shirt and below his navel was a large divot with white pus and red blood festering inside. "It hurts like the dickens. And it's only a matter of time. Anyhow, I'm about done here. It should take a few months to heal, but you'll be okay. And you'll be okay with all of this too."

When the sewing was complete, the man took the hook, wiped some crusted substance off the spike, and readied it. "Now this is gonna hurt and prolly will for a while, but you get use to it." Without warning, he drove the spike into Billy's nub, and he yelped in pain. His throat was welling with tears, but he remembered what he said about being tough. He swallowed those tears and tried to distract himself with another question.

"Don't you ever get lonely out here?"

He let out a long sigh. "Yeah, it does get lonely, but you get visitors pretty regularly. Whether it be human or animal. But if somebody loses their pup, I suppose you could have an animal to keep you company."

He stuffed some cotton inside the black casing that covered the ugly nub to prevent any blood. "Ah, good as new. It will take ya a while to get used to, but you'll get the hang of it."

Billy looked at his new hand, mesmerized, as if it weren't real, but it was real all right. "What will you do now then?"

"I'm done. I've retired. This is my last day." He grabbed Billy's arm and brought the safe side of the hook across his throat and smiled. "Well, kid, good luck," he said, standing and holding out where his hook used to be. Billy clinked his hook on the side of the wood table and winced at the pain from its vibrations.

The old Hookman bent down to exit the shack and turned his head at Billy. "Could you do me one last favor?"

Billy followed him a few feet from the shack, and they stood at a rectangle of a dirt hole six feet deep. "I don't think I can do this," Billy said.

"This or all of this?"

"All of it."

"I'll leave you with the piece of advice my Hookman master gave to me. Believe in yourself and believe in the hook. The hook is not just a new hand. It will guide you to what's right. Listen to it. You'll know what that means soon enough, trust me. Now I've got to go. Goodbye. I love you, kid."

He stood at the head of his grave and yanked on Billy's arm. He stuck the sharp rusted hook into the side of his neck. Blood sputtered and when he pulled it out, the crimson fountain only grew stronger. There was no reaction in his face. He only fell backwards next to his makeshift grave. Billy was taken aback by that final statement. He had only known the guy for a few hours, and he knew love was a word you should only tell somebody you knew and kissed goodnight.

Billy had closed his eyes for the entire event, but he had a job to do. He knelt and attempted a push with his good hand, but this man must've weighed three hundred pounds. Then in his head he heard a faint voice say, "Use the hook." He looked down and nodded as though it were a normal occurrence. He pressed the hook through his shirt but must have entered the meat of his chest. He pulled anyway. He dragged him through the crinkled leaves and cold dirt. Once Hookman was close enough, Billy unhooked and moved, watching the momentum carry him into the hole. Billy re-used the piled-up dirt to cover him.

Once he finished, he looked down at his normal left hand covered in dirt and hook left hand with the same black filth. He was ready to take on this duty. He knew this was what he was meant to be doing. He was The Hookman.

25 Years Later

Bill Thomas sat on the chair made of tree in the small shack in the middle of the woods. He examined a coyote lying on its side with its fur flapped over and its ribcage poking out. Bill had red liquid around his lips like an infant who dove headfirst into a raspberry cake. But this wasn't raspberries.

He felt bad eating animals. Both in an emotional sense and a dietary sense. His large, distended belly hung over the dead animal, and he had his good hand on his forehead. He was crying, and splashes of tears plopped into the coyote's remaining innards.

When he was first handed the job all those years ago, he was gung-ho about protecting his woods and the persons who entered them. He wanted to protect his mother and her home, but once it came around to killing someone, he couldn't go through with it. He had witnessed many things through the years. Everything from a man stabbing a woman twenty-seven times to a different guy chasing a woman between the trees.

Both instances began with Bill running toward them. Then, one of the persons would spot him as the crime was being committed, and the perpetrator would take off running. Bill would freeze and let them get away. He had to be more careful nowadays, since everyone had a camera on their cell phones. Something the old Hookman could not have predicted. If someone got a close-up photo of him, the legend of The Hookman would be over. But one thing Bill would say he was good at was hiding. There were many police investigations over the years and even one with an entire search team, but each time, Bill was able to avoid them.

Bill kicked the coyote, and it stiffly flipped to its other side, which was also torn open and exposed. He was disgusted with himself. He wished for eggs and bacon his mother would make for him back before this hell began. Bill didn't care if the legend of The Hookman ended even if it would be his fault. Bill wished for this whole thing to be over and to go back to his mother and continue his life. He could have been an accountant or a comic book artist, or an author. But with this hook, he wasn't going to be any of those things.

There was one day where he was so fed up with it, he removed the axe that had cut off his arm and was going to swing it and remove the hook and run out of the woods, saying he was attacked by a madman and he needed help. It would have worked if he didn't wuss out. He figured he would bleed out on the way out of the forest anyway. Why was he so afraid of dying when death was already on the menu?

Bill trudged to the edge of the woods and stared at his childhood home. He did this at least once a day. The blue colonial was still standing, and his mother was still living there.

The only days he wasn't checking on his mother were the first few days he was reported missing. They sent search teams in to look for little Billy.

Billy hid in trees, in the shack, and even buried himself in a small hole to be out of sight of the search team. He heard his name being called repeatedly, and it pained him not to return those cries. Especially those of his mother. When they found Billy's blood in the shack, they cut off the search and determined he was dead. He heard the police while he was sitting on a tree branch.

Billy hid out for the next week in case they returned to look for his body, but no one came. He was forgotten and not cared for. That was when he was ready to live the life of The Hookman.

His mother's bedroom was visible from the woods, and he could see her lying in her bed. Every day he wanted to walk inside and tell her he was okay but lost his nerve every time. He didn't want her to scream and attract attention. He also watched as she slowly got over him. She had different men in the house every few weeks, and watching them on top of her in her bedroom where he shared so many memories with her was infuriating to him.

When summer came around a month ago, she had another man to the house, but he had a stethoscope dangling around his neck. He appeared in her room, and the window was open. He didn't even know doctors did home visits anymore.

"The cancer has travelled from your throat to your lungs. It is imperative you begin chemotherapy immediately," Bill overheard the doctor say.

"No, my son is gone. Most of my family is gone. I'm surprised I even stuck around for this long. I want to let it do what it's gonna do." That was his mother. The toughest person he had ever known.

The doctor had nodded at her decision and left.

Bill returned to the house hourly since that day. If he fell asleep, he had this trick to wake himself up and rush over to see her in the window. He wasn't sure if she was breathing or not, but she was still there, and that was what he cared about the most.

A nurse started coming over every day to help her out of bed to use the bathroom or stretch her legs. She hadn't been able to walk on her own for two months now, and it got worse every day. Bill could hear her rattled breathing from outside. He saw the nurse having to be inches away from her to hear what she was saying. She was slowly and painfully on her way out. That was why he decided today to be the day he returned to his mama.

Twenty-five years prior, there had been a key dug in the flowerpot next to the back door. Bill had watched the flowerpot during his mother-spying times and didn't ever see it move.

Bill stepped out of the forest for the first time in so long he had almost forgotten how the full sun coverage felt on his face. He squinted and looked to the sky to feel the warmth on his cheeks. He stayed there for a few minutes, then approached the back door.

He dug through the potted soil, knocking the sunflower—which had been fake—out and found the silver key. He dusted it off on the oversized jeans he had found tied to a tree three years ago. The shirt he had found strewn out on the ground a year before. It seemed like somebody had been keeping him clothed during his tenure as The Hookman. But he figured it was kids getting freaky and leaving their clothing behind.

He slid the key into the hole and the door opened. The gas stove looked a bit rusted, as did the pots and pans, which hung on hooks above the wooden island in the middle, but other than that, the kitchen looked nearly identical to when he was a child.

He continued into the hallway with the dining room on the left and living room on the right. The front door was directly in front of him. He didn't much care for those rooms right now. He wanted to see his mother.

He walked softly up the stairs, skipping steps he knew would creak. He didn't want to surprise her and give her a heart attack, but he also wanted to let her know he was here.

At the top he peered left because he was too curious to know if his room had been turned into a gym or television room. He looked in and his small Zenith TV with his PlayStation attached remained untouched. As did his bed with the orange Nickelodeon "splat" comforter. She kept it the same. There was a lump in his throat, but he swallowed the tears down.

He had his hand on the knob of his mother's room. His heart was working hard, and his ears were pulsating. He had not been this nervous in his whole life. He wasn't even sure why. It was his mommy. She was supposed to love him for his entire life no matter what. And she didn't have much time left, so this was his only chance to see her one last time.

He swung the door open, and he saw the woman he had watched from a distance for so long. Up close she looked much older than he had pictured in his mind. Her face was a roadmap of wrinkles. A brown blanket covered most of her with her arms hanging out. He could see she was in a pink silk pajama dress.

She was not scared. She was not shocked. She surprised Bill by smiling with her cracked lips.

"I knew you'd come back, Billy," she said in a low cracked voice.

Bill smiled back and ran to her. He hugged her, and it felt good to hold her again. He made sure to keep his hook hanging off the side of the mattress. Now he couldn't stop his eyes from watering. He had missed her so much.

"I didn't know if you'd recognize me. I look—well, different," he said, pulling away from her.

"How would I not recognize my own son?" It looked like it was painful for her to speak.

"But how did you not flip out about this?" Bill asked, raising his right hook arm out.

She smiled again and said, "That day you went out with the neighbor boy, I watched you run into the woods with him. I went out and followed you in."

Bill must have had shock plastered on his face.

"I'm sorry, Billy. This is so hard for me to say. But I don't have much more time to get this off my chest. This is something I have been trying and not sure how to tell you for an awfully long time." Her lung rattles and coughing fits returned now. Bill reached out to attempt to give her some water, but she waved him away.

"Ever since you were little, your father and I noticed something was off with you. You were talking to imaginary friends. I know all children do that, but your play time with them was different. You didn't just talk to them, but you answered for them. I figured it was a kid thing and thought nothing of it. But your father—oh, your father—he spoke with a doctor about the situation, and he was advised it was a phase and it would fizzle away when you grew up." She paused and took a drink of water herself. Bill could hear her voice becoming more strained with every word she spoke.

"Maybe you should take a br—"

"No, you need to hear this." She coughed a few more times and continued. "The first issue was you never grew out of it. Eight years old, nine years old, you were still interacting with invisible people. The worst of it came when you were six. We made a mistake and took you on that haunted tour of the city. You were so fascinated with The Hookman story, especially it partially taking place in our back yard. You went to the library and researched all you could. You cut out articles, pictures, and placed them in a scrapbook, which is still in your room right now."

Bill had no memory of the scrapbook or even going to the library for that purpose. He was sure his mother must have been inside and in her bed for too long and had started putting fictional stories together in her head.

"And I know exactly what you're thinking. You have no memory of any of that. Or something else took its place."

Bill was trying to figure out what his mother was saying. What she was trying to tell him.

"At that time, your imaginary friends turned into actions. You would do something wrong. Like breaking the vase in the hallway. You said it was Phillip who told you to do it. Any big event that happened was Phillip's doing. You were so adamant about it for so many years that I believed you. And I still believe you are seeing these things happen that way. But in reality, sweetie, it's not. It's really not. It was one of the reasons your father left. He couldn't handle the stress of your situation. I also kicked him out because he was sleeping with his co-worker. But I couldn't tell you that.

So, I made up a story about him leaving and never returning."

"I don't understand what you're telling me. Are you saying I'm crazy? That I'm a nutjob?"

"No, of course not. But you refused to see a psychiatrist or anybody about the situation, so I don't one hundred percent know what is going on in your head, but I figured out on my own that you take this imaginary person and place them at the forefront of blame of all large situations."

The color in Bill's face was rising to his cheeks now. "That's bullshit." He never expected to ever raise his voice at his mother, especially when she was on her death bed. But there was no way this was true. "Okay, but if you saw me in the woods that day, then you saw I was with that big man with the hook for a hand. He wasn't my imaginary friend, was he?"

His mother looked solemn, and her eyes were welling with tears. "I did see you in the woods, and that was the worst day of my life. That was the day I lost my only son."

Tears started down his reddened face now too. "Then why didn't you come and stop him? Why didn't you save me from that monster?"

She paused and inhaled the biggest breath she could muster. "Because you were the monster in the woods that day."

Bill stood from the desk chair and headed for the door. "You're fucking lying. A liar. My own mother."

"I wouldn't lie to you, Billy. Especially now when I'm dying."

Bill was readying his exit, but he thought he should hear his mother's side of events. "Why? How was I the bad guy?"

"I didn't see you take the knife from the block in the kitchen. When I answered the door and Derek wanted to play, you were having your post-nap snack. But I didn't know you had that knife tucked into your waistline. But I watched you two playing in the back yard while I was doing the dishes. Oh, Billy, I didn't like you being outside because I didn't know what you would do out there. I wanted to keep a constant eye on you, and I felt the window from the kitchen was enough. That was until I saw Derek must have mocked you and ran into the woods. That was when I saw you bring the knife out and go after him."

"That's not how it happened." Bill was in a full sob now.

"Billy, please let me tell this, then you can say whatever y—" Another coughing fit, which seemed to go on forever, came out of his mother. Bill didn't move from the spot he was in. There was no desire to help her. "Please let me finish."

Bill waved his hand as if to say, *Go on.*

"I ran downstairs and into the forest. I watched you stick the knife into Derek's back. Then slice his throat, then his stomach. Then you did something strange. You carved an "X" into his chest. I was appalled. Before this you had showed no signs of violence. You were a good kid, Billy. But then you had a switch-up. You realized what you did and began running back home. But then you went into your imaginary friend speech. I heard your questions and answers to whomever it was you were speaking to. I followed you to a shack a mile away. Your screams made me nervous, and I peeked inside. You were using the kitchen knife to carve your arm off. Now I didn't know how you gained the skills you did, but you sewed it up and stuck a hook in your reaming arm. Where would you get something like that?"

Bill figured the question was rhetorical, so he only silently wiped the tears from his cheeks with his good hand.

"Anyway, I didn't think your obsession would end like that. I didn't think it would end in death. That's why I never stopped your research or collections. After attaching your new arm, you dug a hole for hours. I watched you this entire time."

"Why?"

The question looked to surprise her. "Why what?"

"Why did you watch me do all of this and say nothing?"

"Because you were in a state of mental distress. You weren't recognizing what you were doing. If you only saw your own eyes. They were glazed over, and you were in another dimension. If I approached you, you more than likely would have killed me too. I wanted to wait there and wait for your head to clear and maybe talk you down, but the moment never came."

Bill was somehow calm again and returned to his previous seat.

"After the arm cutting, you walked back to where Derek was and dragged him back to the hole you dug and pushed him inside."

"No, I—it was the hook guy. That's who is in that hole."

"I'm sorry, Billy, but it's your friend Derek."

"You're lying," Bill said vehemently.

"The hole is still there. See for yourself."

Bill shot up from the chair and approached the door to do that. Before he exited, he had one more question for his mother. "I was in that forest for twenty-five years and you never visited or brought me anything or even ratted me out. Why?"

"I didn't need to visit you, Billy. You visited me every night at the edge of the woods by my window. I had to force myself to look away each night, but I enjoyed our couple hours together."

"You knew I was there?"

"Of course, silly. Your mother is not stupid. As for leaving you things. You seemed to gain quite a bit of clothing. Some snacks that were often left on the ground. You think those things just appeared there throughout the years?"

"I had my suspicions, but I wasn't sure."

"And during that initial search for you after Derek's mom reported her son missing, I did all I could to turn the police away from that hole in the ground. They must've stepped over it a hundred times along with searching that shack. When they found your blood in there, they assumed you were killed along with Derek by some crazed lunatic while you two played in the woods. I lied to the police more than I had in my entire life. I did that all to keep you safe, Billy. I love you and so did your father."

Bill wanted to run back to his mother and hug her one last time, but he needed to be sure she was telling the truth. He ran down the stairs and out the back. He returned to his shack and began his frantic dig. He was like a dog who was burying a new toy in the back yard. Dirt was flying behind him and piling on his legs in the crossfire.

He made it the six feet and clinked his hook on something solid. It wasn't a rock but a skull. He removed it and examined it after the dirt and maggots fell off. It was a small skull, much too small to be from a full-grown man. She was telling the truth. He had killed his best friend Derek without even realizing it.

He sat in the hole for hours, talking to Derek and reminiscing about the good times they had years ago. The video games, the board games, the television watching, and sneaking dirty magazines into the house and reading them together. Those were good times, and the past twenty-five years were the worst of his life. He was imprisoned in the woods and inside his own mind. And now his sentence was over.

He buried the skull back underneath the dirt so Derek could remain comfortable in his resting place. Billy looked at the hook and whispered to it. As though his mother would hear him. "I love you too, Mommy."

He brought the blade from one jugular to the next. The blood exited in a waterfall, and Billy leaned back and closed his eyes, ready to be lifted back into the good times with his friend. His friend who was mean but would have stuck through anything with him, even twenty-five years in a forest.

BURN

The Simmons library was typically a melting pot of the haves and have-nots, a mixture of homeless people and the wealthy older residents of the nearby neighborhood. However, right now, the library was dark and quiet. I was given permission by Susan Stevens, the head librarian, and the head of maintenance to stay after closing time and read.

It was nearing midnight now, and I closed the library's paperback of *Fahrenheit 451*. I didn't need to bookmark it, as I had read the Ray Bradbury classic many times before, but I still easily referred to it as my favorite novel of all time.

The Simmons library consisted of three floors. I was on the second floor in the room that held biographies and memoirs. I preferred fiction over those stories, but it was the quietest room and had these long beige tables with red leather cantilever chairs, which were extremely comfortable.

When leaving the biography room, you walked through a larger room filled with computers patrons could use. The twenty-six computers were all shut down now. Beyond the computers and against the walls were rows of fiction reads. My favorite section in the entire library.

I exited in the middle of the fiction/computer space to the swirling staircase, which guided me to the first floor. The only two tasks I was given upon exiting were to shut the lights off—which the night cleaner typically shut off anyway—and set the security alarm. The lights were already off, so I only had to set the alarm on the keypad by the exit.

At the bottom of the stairs, I made it a habit to look left and right to make sure I wasn't locking anybody in here. There were a few times when I would be locking up and one of the many homeless people who frequented this library decided to spend the night. One of the instances caused a big stir and the local police were called. The head of the library was concerned about safety measures and having me inside but ultimately, I was able to continue my nightly reading ritual.

I looked to the left to the room where more adult and YA fiction books sat on shelves of green metal. To the right, beyond the circulation desk was a door leading to the children's room.

I continued straight ahead to set the alarm and exit. But in my peripheral vision I swore I saw a flash of a shadow zoom by. I regularly read horror novels and watched movies when they were shown by the library on Friday nights, even though they were of the tamer variety. So, my mind immediately imagined a demon or monster (*clown*?) roaming the children's section, looking for a snack. But I was in here so often I knew the locals who came in and out at all times of the day, so I wasn't afraid.

"Hello?" I called, taking cautious steps as not to alarm them. "Hello, the library is closed. You can come back in eight hours." No response. No movement. But then again, I didn't initially hear a sound.

I walked through the entryway into the children's room. The walls were painted with artwork from various children's stories. *Horton* to the left and *Cat in the hat* to the right. The skinny books sat neatly on the shelves around the wood desk where the librarian sat during the day. Sometimes when I was exhausted, I would begin to see things. That was my conclusion for this venture.

I shrugged and turned to exit. A man was standing beyond the doorway in the vestibule between the children's room and the front lobby. He was a black man with a strong jaw and few teeth. He was dressed in a long gray trench coat with a white tee shirt underneath and tattered blue jeans. He was wearing the homeless cologne of urine and liquor. What made him stand out was a long scar that ran from his forehead through his right eye, ending at his cheek.

I jumped back and held my chest as though I were going into cardiac arrest. I did not recognize this man as a repeat patron.

"You scared me. I'm sorry, but you can't be in here. I have strict guidelines to follow from the head librarian," I said.

The man did not move. The man did not speak. He only stood there and stared at me. His left eye was brown and looked like a cat's eye. His right eye was closed, and he looked as though he was unable to open it.

"Do you understand? You must leave. Please." I jumped back again when he raised his right arm and pointed at my hand. I was holding the paperback of *Fahrenheit 451* at my waist.

"Oh, yeah. I have already checked this out, see?" I opened the front flap and pulled the due date stamp card out, showing it wasn't due back until—

I glanced at the card and it showed the return date as September 15, 1986. Thirty-two years ago, to the date. But I had watched the librarian stamp this card earlier that day. My constant reading of fiction took me to the world of the unthinkable. That this was some sort of alternate reality or a dream sequence. Maybe this man knew something.

"Did something happen on this dat—" I started to ask, but when I looked up the man was gone.

I would have heard the front door open and close, which was the only way in or out. I did a slow walk-through of the entire library, but I was the only one there.

***

I was back at the library early the next morning at opening where things appeared normal. No strange men wandering. No odd occurrences. So far.

I entered through the front, and I didn't look right at the YA fiction or left at the children's section. I climbed to the second floor. My favorite librarian was booting the computers for the day.

"Liam, so nice to see you bright and early." Vivian had been working at the Simmons library for the past twenty years. She also had an incredible memory. If anyone were going to know a face, it would be her. "Oh, I see you have Fahrenheit out again; what is it, your one hundredth read now?" she said with a chuckle.

I returned with a warm smile. "Only the ninety-ninth."

She cocked her head and furrowed her brows. "You look a bit pale today. Everything okay?"

"If I described someone to you, can you tell me if they ever came into this library?" I asked.

"You seem to recall patrons better than I do, but I can try," she said, pushing her short dirty blonde hair to the right.

I described the man in the trench coat as well as I could to her, making a point of mentioning the large scar.

She removed the pink glasses from her nose, and they swung by her chest on a pink chain around her neck. She folded her arms below her bosom, shaking her head. "I'm sorry, Liam. That doesn't ring a bell."

Then I opened the front cover of my *Fahrenheit 451* copy and removed the date stamp card.

"Also, take a look at thi—"

I was so freaked about last night that I didn't even open the novel after the encounter. But I needed to show someone the date stamp. When I looked at it, it was back to the original dates it had been when it was stamped the day prior.

"No, this isn't right. This was different last night. I swear. I must be losing my mind," I said, placing the card back inside the front cover. "I swear it only had one date on it and it was from a while ago."

Vivian came around the long wood desk and placed her arm on my shoulder. "Are you getting enough sleep, hon?" she asked. It was a normal question I got from the librarians here. They were family to me. My only real family.

"Yes," I said. It came out a bit more aggressive than I had intended, but she didn't seem to notice or appear bothered by it.

The early risers who wanted to use the computers or get some early morning reading in were now shuffling in.

"Did the date have any significance to you?" she asked.

"No, but it was the exact date. Well, yesterday's date anyway. Thirty-two years in the past."

Vivian thought for a second, as if she were doing math in her head, and then I saw a change in her expression. It was only for a moment, but her face blanched to white.

"Excuse me, can you help me find this book?" A man had arrived on my right, holding a torn piece of paper. Vivian ignored him for a second, still looking at me.

"Get some sleep," she said, then turned away, not looking at me anymore.

I left and took her advice.

***

I was back at the library the same night with a mission. Luckily, Brad, the head cleaner, was leaving for the night.

When I entered, Brad held the door open for me and told me to have a good night. I wished the same for him.

I rushed to the third floor. At the top of the stairs was a room that held two microfiche machines. To the right of these machines was a tall cabinet of microfilm.

I searched the years on the front of the drawers and found 1986. I pulled it open.

Next, I fingered through the individual boxes for the exact date. I found September fourteenth through September twentieth and removed it. I powered on the microfiche machine, and a flash of white appeared on the flat screen in front of me.

I loaded the microfilm.

Click.

A newspaper article appeared from the Simmons Times. The front-page article praised the Simmons High school football team for their second win of the season. But this was the fourteenth. I used the knob, and the machine whirred as a blur of black and white whizzed by on screen.

I stopped at the fifteenth.

The front-page article read:

Guns N' Roses performing in nearby Redhill.

I felt deflated.

That was the big news from that day?

Then I thought if something occurred on the fifteenth, it would probably be in the next day's newspaper. I whirred down to the next day.

The big headline on the sixteenth was another article discussing the Simmons High football team. I decided to scroll back up and do a slow stroll through the rest of the fifteenth's paper.

Nothing.

On to the sixteen. It wasn't a long paper, but two pages from the end, a small article was stuck in the top right corner. The headline made me shiver.

Simmons Public Library burns to the ground.

A loud bang forced me to my feet and out of the no-backed plastic stool. I turned to look at the dark stairwell. I was so entranced with getting up there I had forgotten to switch the lights on.

I made the slow walk to the stairs and carefully made my way down and into the large second floor computer room. When I stepped inside, a light from the biography room, where I enjoyed reading, caught my eye. The head cleaner usually shut this off, but he could have left it on for me.

I entered the room and saw a book sitting on one of the rectangular tables. It was *Fahrenheit 451*. The copy I took out. The copy that I didn't bring with me. I opened the front cover and removed the stamped card. September 15, 1986 was stamped in black.

I dropped the novel back on the table, and when I turned, I bumped into the man in the trench coat. I looked up, and his scar remained through his eye, but now his entire face was covered in what looked like acne cysts. These boils were actively bubbling like boiling water. They ran down his neck and as far down his chest as I could see.

When I broke off my dazed stare from his face, I looked around to witness the entire biography and memoir section engulfed in flames. The stories of so many were disintegrating before my eyes.

I ran to the next room, and all the computers had vanished, replaced with shelves of books, also in flames. I had not even noticed I had run through the man in the trench coat.

In the center of the burning novels was a man in a black and white tuxedo. He stood where the long librarian desk would have been. Where I had spoken with Vivian earlier that day.

But was it still the same day? Same universe?

Tuxedo man held a liquor bottle with a white cloth hanging from its mouth. He flicked a zippo lighter, and the cloth was aflame.

"Technology is a comin'. My company is producing computerized software, and it will take over your lives and it will take over books. These fictional books are rotting the minds of our children, but no matter, books will be obsolete come ten, twenty years. These ones you call classics are not; they were dead upon arrival. Books are a poor man's game, and I find it when I see guys like you on the sidewalk reading fictional books when they should be learning something instead, so they can actually get a job. But no, they just sleep on the sidewalk and beg from the rich." The tuxedo man was spouting off but not facing me—he was facing the doors that led to the stairwell. I wasn't sure who he was speaking to, but I was already fed up with him.

The thick black smoke was causing me to choke and burned my eyes. I peered behind me, expecting trench coat man to come from behind, but I could not see a silhouette of anything. The smell of stories burning was the worst part of it all.

Before I could make it to the tuxedo man, a person seemingly appeared out of thin air and tackled the man. His Molotov cocktail flew into the air toward me and smashed, turning the green carpet into a wall of fire. This blocked me off from the two guys fighting and rolling on the floor. More importantly, it blocked me from the exit.

I had to make a quick action as to what I was going to do next. My two options were to stand here and burn or run through the firewall and fight. I chose to run through. The flames seemed to grow higher and hotter once I pushed through, but I made it unscathed.

I pulled the attacking man off the tuxedo man, and he fell backward onto his hind end. I couldn't believe what I was seeing. He was a black man with a scar through his right eye. He had a white tank on but no trench coat. However, this was the same man, only much younger.

Something fell from his jeans' waistband and was on the floor next to him. It was the *Fahrenheit 451* paperback. The same exact one I currently had taken out and the one that had surely burned in the next room over.

I grabbed it from the ground and stared for a few seconds before placing it into my waistband.

I stepped back and watched the only things I loved, the only things that brought me joy in my thirty years of life, disappearing before my eyes. And it boiled my anger. I could feel my fists and jaw clenching nearly on their own.

I approached the man in the tuxedo, who was leaning against a shelf. It seemed the smoke was getting to him as well. I knocked him on his rear end with one swift punch.

I grabbed the young man to lead him out of the library before the entire building collapsed on top of us.

When we reached the stairs, he yanked back on my arm.

"What are you doing? This place is going to come down," I said.

He shook his head, and he had a young but raspy voice. "No. I have no place else to go, and this is the only place I am treated with respect. The only place I am loved. And surrounded by what I love. They let me stay in here after closin' time. They let me take out however many books I want. What else could I ask for?"

"But you will be burnt alive," I said, trying to pull him to the exit.

"Then I will sit down and burn with my brothers and sisters of literature," he said.

The tuxedo man ran past us and down the stairs. I heard the front door open and slam shut. Neither of us even glanced at him.

"That man was right; I have spent my life begging for money, and that's what I will always be known as. But he had one thing wrong. Books are not a poor man's game. I can walk into any library and pull a book off the shelf and walk out the door with no questions asked. As long as I am prompt with returning it, of course. But the beauty of it is that a man or woman who is wealthy and angry, such as him, can do the same thing. That is the beauty of books and libraries such as this one. Free stories for all. And I assure you, young friend, books will last forever."

I was frozen in time, whatever time I was currently in.

"Now get outta here before you miss out on all the good stories you have yet to read," he said.

I nodded at him and shook his hand. It was a firm handshake, which I wouldn't ever forget. I ran down the stairs and out of the Simmons public library as I watched it burn to ashes.

I walked three blocks. I walked past restaurants I had never heard of before, gas stations with prices at $1.00 per gallon, and abandoned buildings that were previously large skyscrapers.

At the corner of the third block, I stopped in front of Simmons bank, and the flat carboard box I had laid out the day before still lay on the sidewalk. I pulled the black garbage bag I used as a blanket over myself and drifted off to sleep.

***

I woke the next morning to bustling downtown Simmons. The current Simmons. I did what I did every morning, grabbed my paperback, and walked three blocks to the Simmons public library. There was the red brick building standing tall and intact. I entered and found Vivian on the second floor.

"Liam, nice to see you," she said. Kind as always.

"You knew that date, didn't you? The day this place burned to the ground."

She looked a bit taken aback, then sighed. "Yes, I studied the history of this place and I found that awful story in an old newspaper. A man was burned alive inside. It is so gruesome and sad. Even sadder is they think somebody had done it on purpose. They said they believed the same person had burned libraries in surrounding towns as well. And was never caught. Who would do such an awful thing?" she said, wiping her forehead as though she were heating up thinking about the fires.

"There are some sick people in this world," I said and waved to her as I walked off to my reading spot. I removed the small paperback of *Fahrenheit 451* from my waistband. I opened the cover page and pulled out the stamp card.

It read: September 15, 1986. All I could do was smile.

I turned back when Vivian called.

"Oh, Liam. I almost totally forgot. I spoke with the head of maintenance and he says he will be short staffed for the next couple of weeks. One of his employees has the flu.

He wanted to speak to you about a part-time job. You'll need to talk with him about the details, though. He said since you were here every night anyway, you may be able to help with cleaning and garbage. He also said if you did a good job, he may hire you for a permanent position. What do you think?"

The smile remained on my face. Hopefully, she took that as a yes.

CONDOR

Even though she was only nine years old—ten in a couple weeks—she knew her Abuelo was dying. She didn't know because of the beeping machines surrounding her, or her Abuelo lying in the hospital bed in front of her, or even the nurses comforting her with false hope.

It was because her mother had been crying non-stop for the past three weeks since he was wheeled into Saint Rafael's hospital. Young Isabella Garcia knew because it was the same way her mother had acted when they fled Colombia from Papi.

Her mother was running her long bony fingers through Isabella's long black hair and had been for the past hour. Isabella didn't feel it since her mind was in a different world than the hospital room. She was remembering all the good times she and her Abuelo had.

Alejandro Martinez had been her father figure for the past two years. He was her rock she could lean on during the most difficult time of her short life. Now he lay supine in a hospital bed, only kept alive by a plug in the wall.

For the first time since he had arrived at the hospital, he had begun to stir under the thin white sheets. Belinda paused the hair brushing on her daughter to approach Alejandro's bedside.

Was he waking up because I came to visit? Isabella thought.

"Papi, are you there? Despierta, por favor," she said, softly touching his cold, wizened hand.

Isabella watched as his brown eyelids shivered and shot open. The whites of his eyes were lined with veins of red. It scared Isabella a bit, but she didn't jump.

"Oh, Papi." Her mother dropped to her knees, rested her head on her father's lap, and wept. Her cries caused a nurse to burst through the door of the small room. After checking his vitals and assuring he was stable, she exited.

"C—ca—" Alejandro began but broke into a coughing fit. Belinda reached across the bed to the tray table and placed the straw between his cracked lips. He sipped for a few seconds, then pushed it away. He began to speak again and still sounded like he had marbles in his throat. "Can I—" More coughing. Another sip of water. "Can I speak to Isabella alone?" he said to his daughter. Belinda looked to Isabella as though she would have all the answers. Belinda then slowly rose from the bed. Isabella stared at the bleeding streaks of mascara on her mother's cheeks.

"I'll clean up in the bathroom," she said and exited the room.

The four white walls made Isabella feel as though she were in a jail, but looking into the dark eyes of her Abuelo made her—as it always did—feel like she was home. Not the home here in Connecticut, but back in Colombia where she had many friends and a father whom she thought loved her. It was where she and Alejandro would play together and sing songs together. It was a great time until they needed to leave.

Alejandro reached a hand to Isabella, and it was shaking as though he were lying in a freezer. Isabella took his hand, and he was cold, freezing cold, but she held on until he didn't want her to anymore.

"When I was a young boy—" He coughed a couple times, then cleared his throat and continued. "In Colombia. I would get into a lot of trouble. I did things when I was your age that were stupid and dangerous. Things that possibly landed me right here." He smiled at her, but it didn't have the same calmness as his other grins. Although Isabella instantly felt his hand become much warmer, as did her heart. "We had a large forest behind my home. Trees as far I could see. When my Mami would make me angry, I would walk out into the woods and get lost. My only friends were—" The coughing returned in great harrumphs. Isabella fed him some water. "Thank you, Nieta. My only friends were the condors." Isabella tilted her head. "Big birds with long wings," he said, and she nodded in understanding.

"One day, mi Mami caught me with something I shouldn't have had, and I ran into the forest. After a few minutes of wandering, I looked up and saw hundreds of them. They were perched on the tree branches. I had not seen something like that before, and I was scared. I tried to leave the woods, but the problem was I got lost on my way home. After twenty minutes I thought I recognized a large tree, and when I rounded it, I ran into somebody. It was a large man, must have been three hundred pounds. I fell to the floor and lay there, staring up at him, not sure what to do. This was when he removed a large machete and struck it down on me."

Isabella shuttered at the thought, but he didn't break from the story.

"I was little and didn't know what to do, so I covered my eyes and scrunched up into a ball and froze. When I didn't feel anything, I uncovered my eyes, and the man was lying inches away, covered in condors. The birds had their talons in his eye sockets and were piercing his stomach and extremities. There were so many to a point where I couldn't even see him. They were pecking and tearing strands of skin from his round tummy so they could reach his insides. One flew away with an intestine in its mouth as if it were a snake. One had his heart. One had his liver. Then they started on his legs and arms."

Nausea was taking over from the detail of the story, but she swallowed it down. A harsh taste of bile. She also noticed his voice becoming clearer, and his coughing was no more. She had hope he was improving, but deep down she knew—and he knew—he didn't have much time left.

"I know that is not a pleasant story, but I want you to know the importance of the condor. Here." He reached under the white sheets, which draped over the bottom half of his body, and pulled out something gold. "I got this necklace for your Abuela many years ago so she could be protected at all times. Of course, heart attacks are not included." He gave a rusty chuckle. "But I want to pass it on to you."

"No, Abuelo. I don't want it," Isabella said in her soft young voice.

He held it out in front of her face. The skinny necklace was chained together, and at the bottom dangled a gold piece.

"You will take it. It is the only way I know you will be safe. See, it's a bird." He took his other hand and held the gold piece in his palm.

She was overcome with unexpected emotion, and tears began streaming down her cheeks. The memories of them together flashed before her as she touched the necklace and squeezed it in her palm.

"I don't want a necklace. I want you, Abuelo," she said, sucking air in between sobs.

"As long as you have that, I will be with you. I will always be watching over you high in the sky. I will be your protector. I will be your condor." He smiled again, and her tears drifted away. She felt comforted by her protector.

***

Two weeks later.

"Feliz Cumpleanos
Feliz Cumpleanos
Feliz Cumpleanos
To Isabella
Feliz Cumpleanos, mi baby."

Belinda entered the kitchen carrying a cupcake smeared with white vanilla frosting on top and one candle jammed into the center. The flame flickered as it sat in front of Isabella. Isabella only sat with her elbow on the table and her hand on her cheek.

"Blow out your candle before the wax gets into the cake, baby," Belinda said, sitting across from her daughter.

Isabella only sat there, staring at the fire stick.

Belinda blew the flame out, and smoke plumed to the ceiling. She plucked the candle out and threw it in the wastebasket.

"Isabella, I know you are still upset about your Abuelo, but he is in heaven now."

Isabella rubbed her neck and held the necklace of the bird her Abuelo had given her the day before he died. Her safety necklace.

"He will always be inside your heart. Forever and ever," Belinda said.

Tears welled in her eyes, but she held them back. She had cried every day before going to sleep for the past two weeks. She willed herself to fight them back.

She nodded at her mother and gathered her bookbag for her walk to school.

Her school was visible from her home if she looked out her bedroom window. It still took her ten minutes to walk there since she was forced to take several back roads to reach the entrance. Otherwise, she would need to leap fences and pace through back yards as she had seen some of the boys from her school do in the past, who lived close to her.

She only had one friend at school, but she couldn't walk with her since she lived in a different town. She didn't mind walking alone, though. She liked to think about all the fun projects and playtime at school.

Today was special for two reasons. It was her birthday, and it was the last day of fifth grade. She couldn't wait for the summer so she could wake whenever she wanted and stay awake until however late she wanted.

She turned left onto King Drive, which was the final road before coming out to the cross street where her school was. The homes on King were one-level ranch style and were in a normal residential neighborhood. It seemed odd for a school to be at the end of this road where people normally watered their gardens and performed other household chores.

"*Isabella.*"

She stopped and turned her entire body around, thinking somebody was calling her from behind. As she whirled around, she knew whose voice it was, and her body went cold on the June day.

"*Isabella.*"

The soft voice was coming from her right. On her right was a home that looked like it didn't belong on this street. It was two stories and stood over the other structures. It was old and decrepit. Vines were strewn from the roof as though somebody were going to slide down them. Windows were non-existent, and the white siding was caked in a poo brown substance. Cracks ran through like a topographical map. The only piece of the home that looked like it hadn't been touched was the front door. It was stark white and clean with no fractures. She had passed this house many times before but was too focused on getting to school on time, so she rarely paid any mind to it. Isabella stared at the door, expecting somebody, anybody, to walk outside, but it remained still.

"*Isabella.*"

This time she saw movement and saw her Abuelo in the window to the right of the front door. He was smiling and waving as he so often did when he saw her. Then he called for her to follow him inside as though he were a teacher wrangling his students, but Isabella noticed with a shiver she was the only one on this normally semi-busy road. The other houses appeared empty.

She took a step toward the home, then froze. Her Abuelo was dead. She knew that. At least, her mother told her that.

There was no wake or funeral for him. The only immediate family he had remaining were Isabella, Belinda, and a few family members from Alejandro's wife's side who had no contact information. Her mother only said he was cremated and placed in a box, which was in their basement. So, the last she saw was him alive was in the hospital room when it looked to her like he was getting better. But her mother wouldn't lie to her about his death. Isabella knew that as fact.

She chose to ignore the calls and her grandpa's ghost and began to walk toward school. Before she could take a step, a flash of something zoomed by her and a wave of air breezed past her face. It was as though a car zoomed by her on the now quiet street. As the flash happened, there was a small tug on her neck. She shot her hand to her collarbone and rubbed frantically. Her necklace was gone. She searched the road and began wandering onto the brown grass of the dilapidated home.

"*Yoohoo.*"

Isabella watched as her Abuelo dangled the gold necklace from his hand, then darted back inside. She knew at that moment this wasn't her Abuelo at all. She didn't know what was happening, but she did know one thing; she was getting her necklace back.

***

She was reluctant to walk through the open doorway but took a step inside. Once she entered, the temperature dropped thirty degrees and the door slammed shut behind her. She instinctively grabbed the door handle to open it, but the handle wouldn't move.

Inside it was dark. The windows at the front of the home, which had been blown out from the outside, were now intact and seemed to be painted over with black paint. She reached her short arms in front of her to feel her way through. She figured she was walking through a hallway since she could feel wall on both sides of her.

She found a door on her right, but it was locked. But she wasn't invested in entering that door, since farther down she noticed a sliver a light. It was peeking out through the bottom of a door in the distance.

She let the narrow walls guide her way to the door with the light behind it. As she approached, she heard music bumping through. The sound of quick maracas and the light drum joined with an accordion, and the calming voice of a female singer made Isabella instantly recognize it as cumbia music. It was the genre of music she heard on a regular basis blasting through the speakers at her home in Colombia. It made her shiver with fear.

Reaching for the door handle, she watched her hand visibly shaking. As her Grandpa would say when she needed to do something she didn't want to, "Rip the bandage off and get it over with." She did that and opened the door. It opened swiftly and she entered.

She entered to an exact replica of her bedroom back in Colombia. Her bed with a pink comforter. Books she received from America stacked on top of her dresser where she kept her many dresses she loved to wear. On her bedside drawer she had a square light, which spun and projected dancing animals in various colors onto the wall. The music was unbearably loud, as it had been when her mother had gone away for her job, leaving her with her father.

As she was swept away into memories, watching the animals on the walls, she noticed somebody sleeping in her bed. But she knew the person wasn't sleeping because the person under the covers was her. Many nights she only pretended to be asleep.

She approached the bed and watched herself from two years ago fake sleeping with the covers pulled to her neck. Her black hair was spooled on the white pillow, and she could see under the heavy blanket she had her knees pulled to her chest. It was only a couple years ago, but it seemed as though she were looking at a different person. Younger, inexperienced, and a little girl who accepted what came to her.

The present-day Isabella jumped nearly out of her white sneakers when she heard the click of the bedroom door. A man entered, being sure to return the door to its frame softly, as not to disturb the fake sleeping girl. The man had short dark hair, which couldn't be styled in any way. He had a scruffy beard of somebody who hadn't shaved in a few days. He wore a ratty wife beater and torn plaid pajama pants.

It didn't appear present-Isabella could smell anything, but the olfactory sense was like a time machine, and she could still remember the acrid stench of liquor and cigarettes. She knew this man well. This man was her father.

She turned to return through the door she had entered, but it was gone. It was only a wall with posters of her childhood idols. She smacked the wall as though it would open some portal to return her to her own world. Her frantic banging would be sure to cause her old self or her dad to notice her, but she didn't care. She needed to be away from him.

"Come on," present-Isabella said, pounding the wall.

She turned to see her father removing the pink comforter and sliding in next to past-Isabella. She ran to the door her father had entered, which she remembered exited to the hallway. She turned the handle, but it wouldn't budge. She threw her body weight—which wasn't much—into the wood door and only fell to the ground, her pink bookbag saving her from any possible injury.

She rose and tried the door again. Tears fell off her cheeks as she threw her shoulder into the door again and again and again.

"Isabella, mi Amorcito. I want to play our little game." She could hear him perfectly as though he were right next to her because this was an image she could never erase. She could still feel his rough, callused hands caress her face while the other entered the bottom of her shirt, touching her stomach—

"Enough," Isabella shouted, but he continued to touch her former self. She approached the bed and tried to pull him off, but her hand sunk through his body. He was a ghost. This was when the fear and helplessness kicked in and she began to panic. She had experienced this once before and didn't want to again.

She sat facing the door, hoping it would open. She covered her eyes and ears to drown out the sounds and her father's noises, but she couldn't. It was already in her head. She could still hear every word he said and every sound he made.

She let out an exhausted and loud rebel yell and heard a click.

The door opened. She hadn't paid attention to what she was walking into, and she didn't care. She leapt through to escape her nightmare.

***

She landed on hard packed dirt. It was like she was pushed from a high cliff or in this case a treetop. It took the air from her lungs for a few seconds, but she recovered and climbed to her feet.

Now she was surrounded by trees. The trees were bare of leaves and waving in the wind. The wind was cold, and her tee shirt and jeans were not the proper attire. She crossed her arms and rubbed her tiny triceps to create some friction. She used her shoulder sleeves to wipe the dried-up tear streaks from her cheeks and began to walk.

To where, she didn't know.

After what felt like a few long minutes, she saw her Abuelo again. His normal pudgy belly, caterpillar mustache, and the cowboy hat he always wore donned his dome. She smiled and started to jog but stopped abruptly. Following him was the reason she was in this place. She wanted so badly to give him a big hug, but she didn't trust this version of him. The only reason she kept on with her small steps was the shimmering gold necklace that hung around his neck now.

"Come with me, Nieta," he said and took off running. She followed past the line of brown oaks and willows. She needed her protection back, even if she needed to take it from her protector.

She pattered through the ankle high grass with rows of trees on either side of her. She cut right, where the path became narrow, following what looked like her Abuelo. She nearly chuckled, watching the way he waddled away from her with his rear end jiggling in his blue jeans like the Jell-O she used to slurp on.

He made another turn, left this time, and when she made it to where he had turned, she ran into something. She thought it was a tree as she lay on the hard, cold ground. But she knew it was too short to be one of the tall trees. She peered into the darkened skies, and a young boy was offering his hand to her.

"I'm so sorry, amigo. I did not see you there. Let me help you up," the boy said, pulling her to her feet.

Isabella looked him over. He wore a white tee shirt with black suspenders tight on his shoulders clipped to blue jeans. And she nearly gasped out loud when she saw the beige straw hat upon his head. She opened her mouth to ask an insane question, but he spoke first.

"You look lost. It's easy to get lost around here. Are you lost?"

Isabella nodded her head. "Where am I?" she asked.

"I-I guess it doesn't really have a name. It's the woods behind my house. I run through here sometimes when my mom gets annoying. Do you ever get annoyed by your mom?"

She didn't hear his question because she was back at the hospital room, listening to her Abuelo tell the story of the—

"It sure looked like you were in a hurry, though. Anything I can help you find? Maybe we can look together," the boy said, shooting her back to reality. Was this reality, though? The boy had never truly answered her question. She didn't want to know which forest she was in, she wanted to know how she got here, but it didn't seem like a sane question to ask.

"I-I guess I'm looking for my grandfather," she said shyly.

"Well, which way did he go?"

She pointed beyond the boy.

"Oh, well, that's back to where my house is. Let's go." He grabbed Isabella's hand and nearly dragged her like a dog on a leash.

Soon after, he was running between trees and making bounding leaps over large roots protruding from the ground and tiny bushes that seemed to appear out of nowhere. After twenty minutes of running, they came to the edge of the forest and looked out to a field of the greenest grass she had ever seen. The grass was as tall as she was and as far as she could see. The only other sign of life was a blue house sitting in the middle of the large yard.

"C'mon…" He paused. "I never asked you what your name was."

"Isabella," she choked out as though a bug had flown in her throat as they ran.

"What a beautiful name. I'm Alejandro. C'mon, that's my home."

He took off, creating a path and splitting the tall grass as he ran, but Isabella only stood there. She was too stunned to move. She had only heard her mother say it a few times, but she knew. She knew her Abuelo's name was Alejandro.

She tried to push away the similarities and followed him through the high grass, then stomped up the white porch steps behind him.

As she ascended, she had a recognition in the far back of her mind that she had seen this home somewhere before, but she pushed the thoughts away again.

"Luckily, my parents left to go shopping, so we have the house all to ourselves." Isabella wondered where a grocery store would be in this area.

Inside the front door to the right was a carpeted living room with a couch facing a brick fireplace. To the left was a white kitchen. She could only see part of a white refrigerator and a sink. In front of her was where young Alejandro had gone. Up the stairs.

"C'mon. I'll show you my room," he yelled from the top.

Isabella followed with butterflies in the pit of her stomach fluttering, warning her about being here.

When she entered his room, she first noticed the posters of soccer players hanging on the blue painted walls. He had a twin-sized bed with a comforter covered in black and white soccer balls. He was rummaging through the top drawer of his dresser next to his cool bed.

"Where are they? A-ha, here they are," he said and pulled out a carton of Marlboro's. Isabella had the instinctive reaction to smack them out of his hand, but she stopped herself. She watched the eight-year-old boy pull the plastic wrapping off and slide the carton open. He pulled a cigarette out and placed it between his lips as she had watched her Abuelo do many times before.

"You want one?" he asked, holding the long rectangular carton out to her.

She vehemently shook her head. "And you shouldn't smoke either. It's really not good for you." She couldn't help herself; she had to say something to help him. If this was her Abuelo, maybe she could somehow save him, but it seemed crazy. But then again, this entire situation was crazy. She only watched on as he struck a match and burned the end of the stick.

He waved his hand to put out the burning match. "Yeah, everybody thinks I'm too young to be smoking. Lung cancer and all that jazz, but the way I see it is you only got one life to live, and it's mine anyway. So, fuck what anybody else thinks. My parents hate me, and I got no friends, so who cares if I die? Nobody would. Am I right?" His voice was changing from a young boy to an older man.

Tears were starting in her eyes, but she wiped them away as she watched him leave the room. She didn't know why the tears were coming, but there had to be a reason.

"I gotta pee. Be right back," he said, cigarette still hanging on his lips. The slam of the door echoed in the small hallway.

Isabella stepped farther into the bedroom. The shag carpet felt through her thin-soled shoes as she made it to his dresser. She took the carton of cigarettes from atop the chest and tossed them out the window, watching them disappear into the tall grass. She walked back to the dresser and opened the top drawer to check and chuck any more possible cancer sticks. But she wasn't prepared to discover what was in this little boy's top dresser drawer.

She saw things much worse than cigarettes. She didn't dare touch the glass pipe with a dark residue in the round bowl at the bottom. She peered behind her, expecting to see Alejandro standing between the door frame, ready to reprimand her for looking through his things. But she sensed she was allowed to do it. Next to the pipe were small baggies filled with powders and a multitude of matchbooks.

She jumped when she heard a loud whooping cough coming from the bathroom. She slammed the top drawer and exited the bedroom. The coughing was incessant, and it sounded as though it came from a deeper, throatier vocal cord of an older man.

"Are you okay?" she asked through the closed door.

"Yes, I-I'm fi-ine," the familiar voice pushed out.

She needed to get him help, so she turned the door handle, expecting it to be locked, but the rusty knob squealed and turned.

"N-n-n." The coughing broke up whatever he was trying to say, but she guessed he was attempting to stop her from entering. She instantly regretted not listening and shielded her eyes with her forearm.

"Oh my gosh, what are you doing, Abuelo?" His name came out effortlessly because it was him. It was no longer the small boy but the grandfather she last saw lying in a hospital bed. Only now he was slumped against the counter underneath the water basin, and to the left of the toilet bowl. The white tee, jeans, and suspenders were strewn in a puddle of cloth in front of him along with his underwear and socks.

He held a silver scalpel and was slicing a neat thin line through his right pectoral. Then another line on his left side creating an "X." Blood ran like a mini river down his round belly and to the white tiled floor between his legs.

"I-I need to—to get this thing out of me," he said breathlessly.

He tore the skin flaps he had created and separated them.

Isabella couldn't stand the sights and pungent smells and turned to leave, but the door was closed and locked from the inside. She pulled and pushed with all the strength she could muster.

"Nieta, please help me with this. Once it's out, I will feel much better. Please." His eyes were tearing now, but not with clear streams. It was black streaks as though he were wearing mascara.

He took his left hand and wriggled it into the gap in his chest. He fished around in there, and the sound reminded Isabella of her mother stirring pasta after the sauce was put in. Alejandro used his right hand to create a bigger hole, exposing a row of blood-stained bones. Isabella continued to wail and shield her eyes from the self-massacre.

"We're almost there, Nieta, but I may not be strong enough," he said, using his dominant right hand to reach inside his opened chest and yank at his ribs. He released a yell that sounded like he had held it in since he was eight years old. His face winced as he tugged and tugged and tugged. Finally, a deafening snap. He let out a sigh of relief and a cackle of laughter she wasn't expecting.

The next few seemed easier to pop and crack apart. At the sound of laughter, Isabella brought her forearm down and saw her Abuelo smiling now as he reached inside his self-induced surgery hole. A black liquid rushed like a waterfall from his mouth as well as his eyes and ears as his evil laughter filled the small room. He made one more far reach into himself and removed a blackened thing, which looked like a shriveled piece of meat left on the grill too long.

"I can breathe again, Nieta. Can you believe it? I can breathe again!" he said, standing with his arms extended towards Isabella. She rolled away and before he could cross the entirety of the small room, he collapsed into a puddle of his own blood.

Isabella shut her eyes and reached for the door, but it had disappeared; instead, the wall had opened, and she fell into a field of tall grass. It looked to be the same she had walked through to get to the home, but the dwelling had vanished.

***

She hadn't decided this, more so her body had, but she was running. She ran through the tall grass, wiping at her tears she was tired of cleaning from her cheeks. The overwhelming scene she had lived through, paired with the memory of her father she had worked for so long to erase, had broken her.

She made it back into the forest of trees, but this time it was different. The trees were still bare skinny arms waving in the light breeze, but sitting atop each branch were large birds. They wore small ugly gray faces, which looked like turkeys Isabella had seen at the zoo. But their bodies were big and bulky. One of them stretched its wings out, and the width was incredibly long. The large black wings with fancy feathers at the ends were mesmerizing to Isabella. It calmed her emotions and she felt safe, even though they painted a daunting picture.

She walked through the shadows painted on the ground of the ugly bird bodies and trees. She watched the birds as she walked on the dirt and studied their movements. As she watched them perched there, she noticed the similar body shape to the necklace charm and what her Abuelo had said to her.

"As long as you have that, I will be with you. I will always be watching over you high in the sky. I will be your protector. I will be your condor."

She stopped and stared at one bird who was picking at its shoulder, then froze and stared at her. She saw through the evil look, and there was a curl behind its beak. It was a calming smile she had received so many times before.

"Abuelo?" she whispered in a soft, hoarse voice.

"Nieta. You made it." For a moment she thought the bird had responded to her, but the voice came from her left. At the end of the row of trees was her Abuelo, smiling and wearing the gold chain, which looked awful on him.

She froze. She had been through the gruesome scene of what he did to himself. Where was she? What kind of universe was she trapped in?

She couldn't trust anybody or anything here. She needed to get out, but she didn't know how. But what drew her closer to him was a smell. A smell that brought her back to Colombia when she was six years old.

It was summertime while her parents were at work and her Abuelo was watching her. He had told her he was going to make her something special. It was special because her parents would never allow it for breakfast. He had reheated rice and beans from the night before and added some eggs, chorizo, and sliced avocado on the side. It was the best meal she had ever eaten, and any time her mother cooked eggs and chorizo, the smell transported her to the special day sitting at the stripped kitchen table, laughing and enjoying the company of her true father figure, her Abuelo.

It was what she smelled now out in the forest. She even heard the sizzling and popping of the meats cooking.

"I made your favorite meal," the familiar broken English voice called from a hundred feet away, but she didn't move. Didn't trust this. But it turned out she didn't need to approach him.

She yelped as the back of her knees were hit by a plastic object, and she was forced backwards where she feared she was falling into another dimension or scene or whatever it was she was traveling through. But she fell back into a chair, which was being pushed towards the smell.

Standing behind her with a big grin was her Abuelo. She recognized the table as the one at her home in Colombia. Her Abuelo appeared across from her, sitting there with half his plate empty.

"Eat, Nieta. It will get cold," he said, pointing with a fork.

She couldn't get up. She wasn't tied down by anything, but she couldn't move from the chair.

"You need to finish your food before you leave the table, you little shit." She peered to her right and her father was sitting there, snapping a chorizo link with his back teeth. He had the white wife beater on and a shit-eating grin all over his face. The wonderful intoxicating smell of chorizo and beans was replaced by the similarly familiar stench of her father's rancid cologne mixed with the cologne he drank with dinner every night.

"Please don't speak to your daughter that way. I'm sorry, love. We want you to grow up big and strong, and food is important." She was now looking at her mother, who had emerged out of nowhere. The forest in the background was slowly fizzing away and being replaced by the Colombia house kitchen.

"If you don't show the kid who's boss, then how is she gonna grow up to be tough? You just don't know how to parent—that's what your problem is."

Whenever Isabella's parents would argue, she would look to her Abuelo for guidance. But he had his head drooped, aggressively shoveling eggs into his mouth. Isabella pushed on the table, wincing and using all her strength, but it was no use. She wasn't moving from this dinner from hell.

Then she noticed something. All three of them were wearing the gold chain around their necks. She lifted her arm and slowly moved it towards her father while he was yelling at her mother. She grabbed hold of the chain, but he grabbed hold of her arm.

"What the fuck do you think you're doing?" he said, squeezing her tiny forearm. His eyes were growing from almonds to meatballs in a matter of seconds, and his mouth was a snarling growl. He lifted her small arm, and Isabella feared her shoulder would pop out of its socket as she hung there like a Christmas ornament.

She was facing her Abuelo, who continued to shovel food into his mouth like a mongrel. Her mother rose from her seat, then was blown back as her father extended his free arm toward her. It was as though a whoosh of air with the power of a tornado exited his hand, and she flew through the plastered wall, leaving a hole the size of a small crater.

Her bastard father held her, so she was facing him. He exposed his missing front tooth and remaining yellow, blackening, crooked molars. "Let's go in the bedroom, mi Amorcito. We have some remaining business," he said.

She began to flail and kick at his bony chest and abdomen, but it was only causing more pain in her shoulder. He kicked the door open and tossed her on the bed. She bounced on the soft mattress.

Her father pulled the wife beater over his head, exposing a chest tattoo that read, "Isabella Mi unico amor verdadero." *My one true love*. Followed by her birthdate.

He continued by unbuttoning his jeans and dropping them to his ankles. She curled on the bed, bringing her knees to her chin, and began sobbing.

He approached, his smile never faltering. He sat on the mattress, the springs creaking. He reached his hand to touch her cheek as she had experienced too many times. It was how he started each time. She thought she had experienced this for the last time years ago, but this wasn't a replay—this was new, this was real.

His crusty hand scratched her cheek, and he blew out a relaxed sigh. As he leaned in to kiss her cheek, she slapped his. It barely moved. He laughed and she watched as his nonexistent belly jiggled mildly. But she also watched—as she was the entire time—the chain moving about his neck.

As he shook off the slap and came close to her again, she grabbed the chain and didn't hesitate to pull it. It didn't come off the first pull, but the bed vanished and turned to the dirt ground. The bedroom started to fade into the background, and the woods took charge as the trees sprouted in favor of walls and dressers. This time the branches grew green leaves on their arms. They were coming back to life, and she knew she was doing the same. As she tugged, she saw something in her father's eyes she had never seen. Fear.

"Adios," she said. The chain broke from behind his neck, and the bird charm fell into her palm. Her father faded away as she rested her head on the dirt, which was happily not as comfy as her former bed.

Her long dark hair pooled around her like a halo. The sky, which had been dark and gray, was now moving rapidly away, exposing a clear blue sky. The condors that had covered the trees flew off in haphazard directions. Isabella viewed it as the most beautiful thing she had seen. She kept the gold chain clasped in her hand and held tightly to her chest as she rose to her feet.

Her heart leaped with joy as she peered left and saw a single door with no frame or walls to hold it in its place. It sat lonely between the rows of trees. And she recognized it. It was a brown dilapidated door with cracks. It was the door that had entered her into this mess. It was the door from the home on King Street.

She ran, nearly skipped, to the door. She had completed the worst thing she had ever been through, and now she was going to be back in the town where her home was with a mother who loved her.

But what if it isn't? the back of her mind called.

What if it was only another path to more painful experiences? Her mind screamed in a panic, but she ignored these calls and ran. She was home free.

That was, until her Abuelo stepped in front of the door. His beige suspenders gleamed over his white tee shirt and clipped to his blue jeans. His straw hat sat atop his head. But she was only staring at the gold chain hanging from his neck.

No, she had that already. She looked at her palm and watched the gold chain convert into a pile of black dust and sprinkle from her hand in a dark blizzard.

"No," her throat croaked. It was happening again. She didn't know what to expect, but it was happening.

"Nieta, it's me. It's really me. I know you've had a hard time since I left you. But you need to hold on. You are a strong young woman, and you have proven that time and time again. You will make mistakes like your Abuelo, but you will grow up to be someone special. I can guarantee you that."

She didn't cry this time. She wasn't out of tears, but she was stronger, and she believed this was her Abuelo speaking with her in some kind of afterlife scenario she didn't fully understand.

He extended his arms to her, and she didn't hesitate to embrace him in the best hug she ever received from him. A hug of ultimate reassurance.

But as she held him, his back became scaled with fine lines, which felt like wrinkles. He had wrinkles, but these were more profound.

She peeled her cheek from his stomach and looked up into a mangled, gnarled face. Her Abuelo's distinct jowl under his chin remained, but it was mashed with her Papi's five o'clock shadow and piercing angry eyes. It also had her Mama's soft features in the cheeks.

Isabella flinched and took a few steps backward. The face was interchanging between the three most impactful persons in her life. Her Abuelo would take over and she would be able to see his soft, caring eyes for a moment, then it would switch to her Papi's snarling grin, then her mother's caring stare. It looked as though they were fighting for who was going to keep the one body. The thing was spasming in what looked to be the beginnings of a seizure while standing. Isabella was only focused on the door behind it. She planned to make a dive for it, and this was her chance.

The thing stepped over to the side, and she ran, turning the doorknob, which jiggled slightly. Then she heard a maniacal giggling grow behind her. It came from an old woman. Isabella turned .

The woman had a chin that stretched five inches beyond her nose. It was spotted with various sized red boils. The woman's teeth were mostly missing, and her skin was covered with craters deep enough to fit multiple marbles. The outfit her Abuelo was wearing was ripped, and its shreds were strewn throughout the dirt, but the gold chain remained, and Isabella knew it was what she needed to escape this mess.

"You can't leave, little missy. You are stuck in here forever." The woman's voice was identical to her laugh, like she had been a smoker for the past sixty years of her life. She ran her bony hands and long yellowed nails through her thin gray hair. She had a quilt draped over her shoulder and held a wicker basket resting on her forearm. "You haven't even finished your meal." She removed a plate with a mountain of rice and beans, but it didn't have the special smell. It smelled like the toilet after you released them from your body.

Isabella gagged at the smell and pinched her nose. Then the evil woman unexpectedly threw the plate at her. She ducked in time to miss the nasty-smelling dish. But when she poked her head back up, the woman was inches away, and she had a full set of teeth, which were razor-sharp triangles. Isabella moved to the left before she chomped on her neck. "C'mon, little missy, I need my meal now," the woman called.

Isabella rolled down a small hill away from her exit, but she knew what she needed. Dangling from the evil woman's neck was the key out of here. And as she was when running from their home in Columbia, escaping the grasp of her father, she had to be brave.

She stood and dusted off her tee shirt and her pink bookbag with unicorn keychain still intact. She was ready.

The day they left Columbia, her father had Belinda on the floor and his hands were choking her. Isabella was cowering in the corner, but when she saw her mother's bulging, hopeless eyes, she knew she needed to reverse that. She took a baseball bat her father kept in the corner and swung, nailing him in the side of the head. He was knocked unconscious, and they ran and ran until they were able to get across the United States border. The United States was their home now, and that's where she was going back to.

She stood inches from the battered-looking woman. The woman grinned those evil molars.

"I'm not afraid of you," Isabella said.

"I can change that very quickly."

The thing grew right in front of Isabella. It grew ten feet in seconds. As she strained her neck, Isabella was reminded of the skyscrapers she had seen when she and her mother passed through New York City.

The thing opened its wide mouth and bent, looking to swallow Isabella whole. Isabella didn't panic as the wide mouth came down upon her. She only looked to her right as if somebody had told her to. There was a large branch. Perhaps remnants of the past world of dead trees. Isabella swiftly bent and clutched the branch with ease. A strength she didn't know she possessed lifted the branch and smashed the monster thing on its cheek. The razor-sharp teeth tinkled to the ground upon impact along with the gold chain.

As she held it in her palm, the woman thing shrank back to normal human size and disintegrated into a black dust.

The lonely door opened on its own, and Isabella fell into the dark hallway of the King Street house. As the door shut behind her, she didn't look back. That was all behind her now, and she was looking forward.

She looked at her palm, and the gold chain lay there.

She exited the home into a chaos of flashing lights and scrambling adults.

"There she is," a man in a firefighter's uniform yelled.

Then before she could form a thought, her mother was sprinting toward her. She fell to her knees and hugged Isabella to a point where she was having difficulty breathing.

"Are you okay? Are you hurt? Where have you been?"

Her mother's questions were rapid, but she wasn't paying much attention to them. Isabella was focused on something not often seen on a utility pole in the streets of Connecticut.

A condor.

Edited by: Sara Kelly

Cover art by: Elderlemon Design

About the author

Joe Baldwin was born and raised in the idyllic state of Connecticut where he received his degree in Criminal Justice. When he is not nose-down in a book you can find him on a long walk beside the roar of traffic or attempting to befriend his pug-tailed tabby cat named Piranha. Joe is the author of Jacob: A Novella.